Waypoint:
Hawaii

Shauna Schober

Chaos Ink

USA

Chaos Ink
USA

Schober, Shauna, 1980-
Waypoint: Hawaii/ by Shauna Schober
–1st ed. 2012
ISBN-10:0615726836
ISBN-13:978-0615726830
[1. Adventure-Fiction. 2. Geocaching-Fiction. 3.Schools- Fiction.
4. Interpersonal Relations- Fiction. 5. Oregon (State)-Fiction.]
12 11 10 9 8 7 6 5 4 3 2 1

Printed in the United States of America

DEDICATION

In loving memory of Ethan Jostad.

www.ethanjostadfoundation.org

"Our mission at the Ethan Jostad Foundation is to provide smiles on the faces of children battling cancer. We accomplish this by sending toy packages to children, providing families with financial assistance, raising awareness of childhood cancer, and funding research to help find a CURE. Through our Foundation and the memory of Ethan, we will continue to spread awareness for childhood cancer. It is the leading cause of death for children under the age of 15. On average 36 children and adolescences are diagnosed with cancer every day. Despite these facts the research for childhood cancer is significantly underfunded. We know that the key to change starts with awareness for which we will continue to advocate through this website and our fundraising efforts."

No matter where life takes you - enjoy the journey.

~S.S.

ACKNOWLEDGMENTS

Special thanks to David for being my rock and loving me unconditionally. Stephanie for continuing to fix my errors without any compensation, Steve and Karen for supplying me with research material, Zach for sharing with your teachers, Paul for continuing to support my dream. Catherine, Matt and Lil' Bub, for never allowing the oceans between us to be too big. And of course all the fans who have so patiently waited.

An extra special thank you to Mrs. Stone's 2011-2012 fourth grade class at Jewett Elementary in Central Point, Oregon. These students chose the location of the fourth book in the Waypoint Book Series. ~P.J. A, Hope B., Dalton B., Brenden B., Nathanael B., Tyler C. Grant C., Cassidy C., Bruce C., Tanner D., Austin D., Madelyn F., Chazz F., Rhaden G., Mayra G., Ashtyn H., Ethan H., Alyssa J., Sarah M., Alexis M., Connor M., Mandy M., Anna M., Taylor P., Amber R., Emmanuel R., Javonte S., J.J. T., Jacob W., Kayana W. , and Averi Y. I strongly value your feedback and awesome ideas!

This is a work of fiction.
None of the waypoints in this book lead to actual geocaches.

Waypoint
Hawaii

1

Ben's hands shook uncontrollably, never before had he been so scared, so terrified, so angry. This was all his fault, had he never won the contest in Oregon and then ventured to Alaska his entire family would be totally safe. Now his family was in jeopardy, his parents and Trent were being held hostage in Oregon, while he, Megan, and Lacey were being held hostage in Hawaii as they led Henry to each geocache. With every stop Henry was becoming more and more irate. Ben had tried to explain that this wasn't some huge treasure hunt; he had tried to explain that this was all just a game. Henry wouldn't believe him though, even though he knew nothing of the deed to the gold mine. Ben, Lacey, and Megan had decided it would be best to keep that to themselves. They didn't know if it was real, so why entice this jerk more, they rationalized.

"It would be easier to open this thing if you'd take the gun outta my back." Ben complained to Henry. He swore he'd have a round bruise from the barrel of the gun as soon as this nightmare was over.

"Just open it and quit your whining!" Henry snarled. He scratched the dark brown scruffy beard on his neck. His bandages were still fresh from the ice cave collapsing on him. This was the only time Ben had ever wished that someone would have died, and still he felt guilty for wishing that.

Ben's hands continued to shake. They were in a

small alcove on the memorial of the USS Arizona, in Pearl Harbor on the island of Oahu in Hawaii. After realizing the geocache was on the memorial they took the tour boat out and listened to the guide talk about that day in 1941 when 1177 crewmen were killed on the ship below the memorial. This ship had become their grave, a lump grew in Ben's throat as he thought about it, all of those lost lives, all of those souls resting below him, a shiver ran up his spine. As he shook the barrel of the gun pressed deeper into his flesh. He forced himself to concentrate, he wouldn't put it past Henry to add one more body to this memorial.

The key turned easily in the small metal box, as it popped open Ben saw a familiar brass key and a small note from the Cache Master. He unfolded the paper carefully and read it out loud, "*'Many of my dearest friends rest below you at this time, I was a lucky one. Take the time in this place to acknowledge them, take the time every day to think of those who gave you the ability to do as you please.* Signed, *The Cache Master.'*" Ben rolled the key in his hand and then read the coordinates out to Lacey so she could enter them in her cell phone. "We have 21°24'06.54" North and 157°49'32.16" West."

"Okay, it's not too far from here," Lacey mumbled. She swept her long brown bangs out of her face. Fear had totally overcome her, her eyes were swollen from crying, and even her voice was shaky with panic.

"Well, let's get on with it, then!" Henry demanded. The group turned and walked back to the small boat that would take them back to the main office of the memorial. As they sat and waited for the rest of the people from the tour to join them Ben thought of what the Cache Master had written, and he thought of all those sailors who had died and were buried in a watery grave below them. As he rested his eyes deep in thought a vision of bright blue wrinkled eyes came into his mind. These eyes floated in a black space, swirling long gray hairs misted through the vision and a raspy voice inhaled deeply then said, "Breathe." Ben jumped at the sound and looked around to see if anyone else had heard it. He quickly rubbed the goose-bumps from his arms and tried to find peace in the vision. He took a deep breath as instructed by The Keeper. Slowly the fear and anxiety melted away and, if only for a moment, Ben felt peace.

The tour boat filled slowly once again and then made its way back to the main memorial office. The group unloaded and headed toward the van Henry had rented to take them around the island. Had it not been for their parents being held hostage in Oregon, Ben and Megan would have escaped long ago, but they knew this was their only hope at protecting their mom and dad.

Henry followed the instructions Lacey read off her cellphone from the GPS map, after a few minutes they arrived under an overpass to a freeway. They parked in a small lot and climbed out of the van, then made their way to where the GPS indicated. As they walked up a gravel path they came to a large gate labeled, "Haiku Trail" under the name was a huge sign that read, "Closed to the Public, No Trespassing".

"Well, what do we do?" Megan asked. She looked to Henry, trying to be as respectful as possible, and fighting every urge she had to kick the guy in the crotch and make a run for it.

Ben and Lacey looked around the gate, looking for anything that would resemble the geocache. Lacey was digging through some shrubs when she called out, "Found something!" She lifted a small metal box and held it while Ben opened it with the key from the USS

~ 3 ~

Arizona. It popped open easily, and Ben removed a small slip of paper from inside.

"There's no key in this one," he said to Henry. Henry glared and grabbed the box, not believing what Ben was saying. Ben began reading the note from inside the box, "'*Follow the stairway to heaven, be slow you have 3,922 stairs to go.*' That's a lot of steps," Ben acknowledged.

"Better get moving then!" Henry growled.

They began hiking a small trail that led through dense foliage and finally came to the first of the stairs, looking up ahead they saw the stairs extend up into the clouds and mist above them, it was incredible and eerie all at the same time. The stairs and railing looked as though they were semi new, although the weather had aged them, the cool salty mist from the ocean aided in the bleaching of the wood and corrosion of the metal. As they gained altitude the wind picked up, blowing Lacey and Megan's hair all around, Ben pulled his baseball cap tighter onto his head.

After about twenty minutes of climbing a loud yell came from below, the group looked behind them and saw four armed men running up the stairs from below, they looked like they were in the military. Ben grabbed Lacey and Megan's hands and pulled them faster and faster up the stairs, "Stop!" one of the men yelled. They continued to run, jumping two and three steps at a time, as Ben looked back he could see that Henry was apprehended.

"Keep going!" Ben yelled to the girls. They were panting and out of breath and could hear the footsteps of the armed men coming up from behind them. Soon they were in a dense, thick mist. Their visibility was low and an eerie howling of the wind took over the quiet of the abandoned mountain. As they came to a deep ravine and a metal and wooden rope bridge, Ben hopped the handrail at the edge and motioned for Lacey and Megan to do the same. The men following couldn't see them in the thick fog. They hid in some shrubs at the edge of the ravine, trying to control their breathing.

"If we get caught, we can just explain that Henry has kidnapped us," Megan whispered.

"If we get caught, all this is over though, and we might be arrested, those guys look pretty serious." Ben replied. "Let's just wait it out, we can hide until dark and then finish the climb." They sat and waited, quietly. They heard the pounding footsteps of three of the men cross over the bridge above them. It swayed with their movement, just the thought of crossing it terrified Ben, but he knew he had to. Ultimately, he knew finding the final geocache was his only release from this nightmare. Only then would Henry leave them alone; and only then would he know that he would be fulfilled and satisfied that it was all over.

This entire thing had been exhilarating, it had been terrifying and dangerous, but deep down Ben loved the chaos, the challenge. He felt as though this would probably be the only chance in his entire lifetime to truly have an adventure. He knew that even though they were all in danger, somehow they would all be okay.

As the rope bridge above them slowly stopped moving, they all lay back in the brush and decided to wait a while longer, they figured the men would realize they weren't ahead of them any longer and turn around and head back down the stairs. As they waited they whispered, this was the first time since arriving at home with their parents that Ben could talk openly with Lacey and Megan, since that horrible day they had been under constant supervision by either Henry or Eddie.

"So, what's our plan?" Lacey asked quietly, "I mean once we find the other half of the deed to the gold mine in Alaska?"

"I say we split all the money," Ben whispered.

"What about Henry and Eddie?" Megan asked.

"I'm hoping we can take care of them on this trip, or at least Henry, Eddie seems like he's just doing what he's told," Ben responded.

"What do you mean 'take care of Henry'?" Megan asked.

"I mean, we somehow get rid of him, and if that means permanently then that is what it means." Ben's eyes grew dark as the words quietly came out of his mouth.

"You wanna *kill* him?" Lacey gasped.

"No, not us personally killing him, but if something happened and he ended up dead I wouldn't feel too bad about it, I mean the guy is holding us hostage, he's had a gun in my back the last week! I'm saying *if* while we're tracking the clues down he has a heart attack or is eaten by a shark or something, well…that's just nature taking it course." Ben smiled mischievously.

"Wow, okay, I guess that makes sense," Lacey replied, "I'm just not killing anyone."

"Yeah, yeah, me either, we just have to lose this guy, permanently." Ben closed his eyes and relaxed, he was hoping that Henry would continue to be apprehended by the guards, and that they could somehow make their escape. They could get to the top of the mountain, find the next geocache and maybe be done with this whole thing. The three settled in for a few hours, waiting to hear the footsteps again of the guards crossing back over the bridge. Darkness began to set in, and they were high enough on the mountain that a chill mixed with the thick fog, as the wind howled through the ravine. In the dark it was frightening, but not nearly as scary as having Henry hold them at gun point.

Finally, an hour later, they saw lights shining over the top of the rope bridge. They heard the men crossing back over. Ben, Megan, and Lacey froze in place as the beams of light got closer and illuminated the ground around them.

The men were searching for them still, but seemed intent on getting down the mountain. Ben heard one of the men as he talked with his friends, "I think they went down the other side of the mountain once they got to the top. There wasn't any damage up there, so I say we head back. We'll take the man into custody and see what we can do with trespassing charges. The kids would be hard to charge anyways."

"Yeah, I say we call it a night," another man replied. The beams of light from their flashlights slowly faded and then once again everything was black, except the crescent moon over head in the starry sky. Ben looked at Lacey and Megan. Lacey held up her hand indicating she wanted to wait at least five more minutes before coming out of hiding.

Five minutes seemed like ages as the wind continued to howl ghost-like as it swirled around them. Megan shivered from the cold breeze and tucked her arms into her shirt. Finally, Lacey stood and made her way up to the railing of the stairs, seeing no one in either direction she motioned for Ben and Megan to come out of the shrubs. They climbed over the handrail and started to walk carefully over the rope bridge. It swayed with every step. They each slowly stepped from one wood plank to the next. The bridge was only two-feet wide; as they advanced it bowed even lower to the ground under their weight. Ben tried to only look ahead and convinced himself not to look down. He had made that mistake as they first entered the bridge and was still recovering from the nauseated feeling that had overtaken his gut.

As they reached the other side of the ravine, relief was evident on their faces. They couldn't see very far ahead but saw that immediately the stairs started again. Megan sighed loudly then said, "Well, we have about twenty-nine-hundred steps to go."

"What?" Ben and Lacey both asked.

"We were right around one-thousand when we hid, I've been counting," Megan clarified.

"Seriously? Jeez, this is gonna take forever!" Ben complained. The group started up the new set of stairs, in the dark the steep stairs were even more intimidating, suddenly the sounds of wildlife combined with the wind made them jump and cringe in fear. As they advanced, it appeared as though they were getting closer and closer to the crescent moon that filled the sky. After another fear-filled hour they were finally at the top of the enormous mountain.

Standing on top, looking totally deserted was a small concrete building and a tall radio tower. It appeared to be out of use as no lights were on. The entire place was pitch-black, only the moon and the millions of tiny lights below from the surrounding cities provided any source of light. It was as though they were lost in space.

As they crept around the building they searched for the geocache. The weeds and shrubs on the ground made being stealthy rather difficult as the tripped and plodded through the thick vegetation. After they circled the cement building they carefully made their way to the base of the radio tower, the thick metal legs were also corroded from the salty sea air and the harsh weather elements so high on the mountain's peak. Lacey noticed that one of the steel beams of the legs of the tower had an object on it, close to the base, almost hid entirely by the vegetation.

"I think I found something," she whispered loudly. Ben and Megan carefully advanced toward her. By the time they made their way to her she was holding a small metal box, which matched all the previous geocaches. Ben removed the key from his pocket and the group sat on the moist vegetation covering the ground with the radio tower rising above them.

Ben slid the key into the keyhole, turned it a fraction of the way around and the box popped open, inside was another key, he quickly pocketed it then searched the rest of the box for any clues, there were none. "I guess this isn't over yet," he sighed.

"So what are we gonna do now?" Megan asked.

"I say we go down the back side of the mountain, find a road and a place to stay for the night and then track down the next cache tomorrow." Ben answered.

"What about Mom and Dad, and Trent?" Megan asked as she stood.

"Let's call the police in Central Point, Henry isn't with us, so they can go rescue them and take care of Eddie. We can call and tell them that we're safe now and they can come meet us on the island or something." Lacey said.

"Okay, I think that's a good idea, let's get down the mountain first and then find the phone number for the Central Point Police, we could even go to the police here and have them call for us." he replied.

Ben stood, just as Lacey was standing a loud boom filled the air, they all crouched low and covered their ears. It echoed through their bodies, suddenly the sound was bomb-like and the entire structure above their head shook and illuminated as a burst of blue lightning flowed down the steel structure. The hair on all of their heads stood on end as they ran to the cement building. The sound was deafening and the ground shook. They ran further away from the structure as the vegetation on the ground around it caught fire, just as they rounded the corner to the cement building and were heading to the edge of the mountain side Lacey screeched to a halt and screamed. She turned as she tried to run away from what had frightened her, as Ben watched her he couldn't imagine what could be more scary than the lightning strike and fire, as she got closer to him he realized immediately what it was. He tried running but was stunned as he watched a thick heavy hand come down on Lacey's shoulder and pull her to the ground.

2

Ben, Megan, and Lacey stood handcuffed at the top of the mountain. Three guards asked them various questions about why they were here and why they ignored the signs and trespassed. Lacey was explaining that Henry had kidnapped them at gunpoint and forced them to go through the gate, tears poured down her cheeks and she sniffled loudly trying to control her running nose.

"We did find a hand gun on him when we searched him earlier, he's still in custody. You guys did a good job of hiding, we had scoured this place earlier, unfortunately our commander made us climb all the way back up here to look for you again when we came back empty handed the first time." The guard explained.

"We only ran because we felt it was the only opportunity we would have to get away from Henry," Lacey sobbed. "His partner is holding their parents and my boyfriend hostage back in Oregon; they think we have like a treasure map that will lead them to gold or something."

"Really? Well, let's get you guys back down to headquarters and we'll get this all taken care of." The guard smiled shyly at Lacey and then spun her around to un-cuff her.

Ben looked to Megan and sighed loudly, "Almost over." He smiled at his sister.

"I just wanna make sure Mom and Dad and Trent are okay before we go anywhere else." Megan said quietly.

"Me too, Meg. Me too." Ben turned so he could be un-cuffed next. Then the guard moved to Megan and unlocked her cuffs, they all rubbed their wrists, trying to massage the pain away from their bones after the tight metal had bitten into their skin.

As they hiked down the stairs Lacey talked with the young guard who was walking in front of her, explaining geocaching and how they had been on a trip to Alaska where they first met Henry and Eddie. Ben and Megan followed quietly, not wanting to add any details that weren't necessary. The guards had radioed their captain and given him the information about their parents and Trent, they assured them that they would be safe, and as soon as they were Ben and Megan would know about it.

A huge weight had lifted off Ben's shoulders; he had felt so guilty that everyone was in so much danger all because of him. He had also felt guilty that even though everyone was in danger he was still enjoying this crazy adventure.

❧

The morning sun bounced off the bright white side walk and blinded Lacey. Ben and Megan had just spoken with their parents, Eddie and Henry had both been arrested, and now everyone was finally safe. Soon Trent and their parents would be on a flight to Honolulu and would meet them at the hotel that evening.

"So, let's get this next key done and then we'll meet Mom and Dad tonight." Megan beamed.

"Are you guys sure? Once again this is turning into a nightmare." Lacey said.

"Hey, the bad guys are gone, the nightmare is over. I say we go, have some fun, see some sights, meet Mom, Dad, and Trent tonight and see what we find. If we can get to the other half of the gold-mine deed then we can figure out how to get the gold from it." Ben walked backwards in front of the group while he talked and tried to convince his aunt.

"Let's figure out where we're going first, I guess." Lacey said as she pulled her phone out of her pocket.

Ben removed the brass key from his pocket and read the waypoint to his aunt, "We have 22°12'01.33" North and 159°36'52.28" West."

"Well, that's not even on this island, we're gonna have to fly there, that's on Kauai." Lacey showed Megan and Ben her phone.

"Let's get to the airport then, if you use your credit card, we can have United Cellular pay the charges. They are gonna be getting Alaska and Hawaii out of this deal so they should be extremely happy." Ben waved his hand at a taxi cab, ushering it to the curb.

৵৽

Megan and Ben woke as the plane came to a landing on the island of Kauai, they had looked more into where the waypoint was taking them; it appeared to be on the coast, potentially in the water.

The group beckoned another cab and gave the driver as much information as they could, showing him a map on their cell phone, "Looks like you're going to Pirate's Cave." The cab driver informed them. "You'll only be able to access that by kayak or tour boat, it's a two door cave, massive in size, almost twelve-hundred feet long." He merged into the thick traffic exiting the airport. "I'll take you to a kayak rental place I know."

The cab ride was quick, being on a small island, definitely had its benefits, especially after how long each trek was between waypoints in Alaska. Lacey had barely settled into her seat by the time they arrived at the kayak rental shop. She paid the cab driver and thanked him then exited the car.

Renting the kayaks proved easy and they got full directions on how to get to the Pirate's Cave, as well as an underwater camera and snorkeling gear. They weren't sure where the geocache would be located so they figured they better be as prepared as possible. As the shop owner dropped them off and unloaded the kayaks they all put on their life jackets and prepared for an hour kayak trip to get to the cave entrance.

They each launched their kayaks off the white sandy beach and hopped in as soon as they were in deep enough water. The incoming waves were hard to cut through, it took some maneuvering and a lot of paddling, but once they had cut through them the rowing wasn't nearly as challenging.

As they pulled their paddles through the crystal blue waters they could see the amazing coral and fish swimming happily below them. A large turtle came up for air right next to Megan's kayak; she reached over and slid her hand down its shiny, glossy shell. The coastline here was incredible, large mountains gave way to old lava formations and sea caves dotted the edge of the ocean all over the place. Water splashed into the caves and then poured back out and over the rocky beaches. The air was crisp and warm, nothing like the coasts of Oregon and Alaska, this was truly paradise, Ben thought.

As they rounded another outcropping of volcanic stones that had formed a beautiful formation in the water they saw the entrance to a large deep cave. Ben pulled his phone from his pocket and checked the map; the GPS indicated they were only one-hundred feet from the location of the geocache.

"This way," Ben announced as he rowed faster, ignoring the pain radiating through his arms and upper body. As they approached the entrance to the cave the water became choppier and harder to navigate. They slowly advanced toward the opening and heard the eerie sounds of the ocean water echoing out of the large sea cave. The water became darker and darker as they approached the entrance. As they pulled into the large opening of the cave, suddenly they understood why it was called Pirate's Cave. It was large, dark, and winding, and about seventy-five feet in front of them poured an enormous waterfall, directly out of a hole in the ceiling. Sunlight shone through the skylight, creating a creepy ray of light that beamed into the water, illuminating the sharp rocks below.

The sound of the waterfall was almost deafening, it splashed and echoed throughout the cave, in combination with the waves, this created an even more treacherous current to navigate. "Let's pull over to the wall by the waterfall," Ben yelled. Lacey and Megan followed his lead as he tried to maneuver carefully against the wall. He checked his GPS once more and sure enough the waypoint pointed to the waterfall. "Our next cache is somewhere around the waterfall!" he yelled again.

As the water splashed over the top of them they all held the sides of each other's kayaks so they wouldn't become separated. "You wanna get out and try to check it out, Ben?" Lacey called over to him, wiping the relentless splashes of water off of her face.

"Rock, paper, scissors?" Ben called over, clearly a little nervous about the potential of getting caught in the waterfall's powerful shower.

"Oye…okay, one-two-three!" Lacey yelled as she pumped her fist, and then extended her hand flat. "Ha! Paper covers rock!" she smugly called over to Ben who had decided on rock.

"Ben frowned then grabbed onto a large boulder at the edge of the cave. Megan continued to hold onto his kayak as he carefully climbed out and pulled himself onto the slippery rock. He used his hands and feet and advanced over the stones with caution, the relentless flow of water made it hard to concentrate as he had to keep clearing his blonde hair from his eyes. This was like being sprayed by five fire hoses, Ben decided.

He continued to move slowly, holding onto the stones and balancing against the wall of the massive cavern. As he got closer to the waterfall all other sounds were drowned out by the enormous flow of crashing water. He squeezed up against the wall and came to the back of the waterfall, the pressure of the water pouring over him was almost drowning, there was no way to keep it from his face at this point. He looked around as best as he could, using his hand to shield his eyes. As he looked up to the beam of light he saw a familiar dark metal box at the top of the waterfall, resting on a small ledge that was protected by a larger ledge above it, which caused the water to cascade inches from the small ledge.

"Really!?!" Ben called out with frustration. "What is up with this guy and his geocache locations? Uhgg!" he growled in annoyance and fear. He moved to the side of the waterfall once again and motioned to Lacey and Megan to look above them, pointing to the geocache.

Lacey's eyes became huge with worry as she focused in on the box. She shook her head in frustration for Ben, "Wanna use one of the paddles?" She called over to him. "We could knock it off the ledge if you just climb a little ways up!" Ben thought for a second, then nodded his head in agreement and moved down the slippery rocks to get his kayaking paddle.

As he came back to the wall to the side of the waterfall he tucked the paddle tightly under his armpit and began to test handholds and footholds. Everything was slippery with algae and slime. He dug his fingers into the slimy coating on the rocks and began to pull himself carefully up the edge of the cave wall. With every inch panic filled his lungs. He tried to tell himself over and over to continue breathing, to stop listening to the voice of fear in his mind. Surprisingly, that voice was even louder than the crashing water next to him.

As he moved up two more steps, he came within reaching distance of the small metal box. He squished himself as close to the cavern wall as possible trying to get his balance as he wiggled the paddle out of his armpit. He looked down and instantly became nauseated as he realized he was about eight feet off the ground. He quickly shook the fear from his eyes and returned his gaze to the metal box. Shakily, he stretched his arm out toward the ledge. The paddle proved hard to maneuver as there was so much weight from most of the length being away from Ben's arm, his muscles burned as he continued to hold onto it.

He stretched it further and finally the plastic end of the paddle bumped the box. Unfortunately, it pushed it back farther on the ledge, Ben groaned under his breath. He tried again, this time using more of his body to push the weight of the paddle over and behind the box. As he did, it gave way and was knocked into the flow of the waterfall. Ben turned his head and watched the box fall and bounce into the sea water as the waterfall pushed it over the rocky outcrop. "Shoot!" Ben called out, as his frustration took over, he forgot about the paddle in his hand and as it moved into the strong flow of the waterfall the force was too great. The water pushed the paddle down quickly, Ben's arm pulled with the force and before he could think to let go he was being pulled off the wall.

From Lacey's view he seemed to fall in slow motion, and then suddenly a slap sounded through the cave as his body hit the slippery rocks below. Lacey screamed in a panic and jumped out of her kayak, she quickly climbed onto the rocks and moved to Ben's side. Megan followed, but as she exited she pulled the kayaks up so they were resting partially on the rocks. She ran carefully to Lacey's side.

Lacey was shaking Ben's body, he was face down on the rocks, despite all of her first aid training Lacey rolled his body over, and then let out a loud cry as she covered her mouth. Panic took over and all she could do was stare at his lifeless body and at the bright crimson liquid that poured out of his forehead and right eye.

3

Lacey held her fingers to Ben's neck, checking for his pulse. She felt the gentle thump under her fingers, indicating he was indeed alive. Megan grabbed her t-shirt from her kayak; she had taken off earlier in order to snorkel. She handed it to Lacey, who folded it and tightly pushed it against Ben's wound covering his temple and eye. She then had Megan hold the t-shirt in place as she removed her belt and wrapped that around as tightly as possible to secure the t-shirt in place and apply pressure, hoping that the wound would stop bleeding.

"What should we do?" Megan asked as they sat next to Ben on the cold, slippery rocks.

"Well, one of us needs to stay with him, and one of us should get the geocache."

"Seriously?" Megan questioned.

"Ben will be ticked when he comes to, if we let that thing get away, c'mon, you know how he is." Lacey encouraged her niece.

"Okay, I'll get my snorkeling stuff on." Megan stood and carefully maneuvered over the slippery rocks once more as she retrieved her gear from her kayak.

The water churned at her feet, sloshing and splashing on the rocks that she stood on, she looked around the massive cavern, hoping the current hadn't already swept the geocache out to sea through the other exit in the cave. She took one step into the water and then allowed herself to fall. The water, while rough, was warm and inviting. There was a definite undertow and swimming in this cave would be more challenging than in the open water, but she knew she had to.

She looked up to Lacey who was rubbing Ben's head, moving his hair off his face to prevent it from staining even more from his blood. Lacey gave Megan a thumbs-up, Ben was doing okay. Megan slipped her mask on and put her mouth piece in, then slowly went under water.

Brightly colored florescent fish swam all around the rocks at the bottom of the cave. There were so many, Megan almost gasped. Along with the fish were turtles, everywhere, some were tiny, others must have been close to one-hundred pounds, she thought. She moved easily through the warm water, the current was easier to deal with from below the surface, she just had to remind herself to not sink too low, or she would breathe water in through the top of her snorkel. As she pulled herself through the water she could see where the sunlight shone through the surface from the hole in the ceiling of the cave. It illuminated a small area that flourished with kelp and seaweed. Small fish darted in and out of the green oasis. The rocks shimmered with the sunlight dancing through the water, it looked absolutely incredible. She continued on her search and finally saw something else shiny along the side of the cave bobbing in the water by some large boulders. She moved closer to it and verified it was indeed the geocache. She swam as quickly as she could and then swiped it from the water. She raised her head quickly and hollered to Lacey through her snorkel, "Found it!" her voice was muffled, and sounded more like humming then speaking.

She tucked the box in her arm like a small football and worked her way back through the water, as she was crossing the center of the cave she felt something soft touch her leg, she giggled thinking it was just a fish who had gotten too close, then bobbed under in order to check out the brave fish who had caressed her skin. She turned quickly, and then screamed into her snorkel, there floating under her was a human hand. She plunged up thru the water and screamed again then quickly began swimming to Lacey. As she reached the rocky shoreline she handed the geocache to Lacey and then climbed onto the rocks, "There's a body!" she screamed.

"What?" Lacey questioned standing next to her niece.

"A body! It's stuck in between some rocks in the middle, its arm and hand are floating and it touched my leg!" Megan did a full body shiver as the thought freaked her out once more.

"Like a person?" Lacey asked with as much fear in her voice as Megan.

"Yes, like a person, a guy! A *dead* guy!" Again Megan did a full body shiver.

"Oh my gosh, okay well Ben isn't awake yet, I say we call 911, we can get him help and tell them about the body…oh yuck…I'm so sorry I had you swim in here!" She grabbed Megan and hugged her tight.

"It's okay…just uh…freaked me out!" Megan

replied. Lacey pulled her phone from her shorts pocket and dialed 911, she explained to the operator what had happened and where they were, within a few minutes a speed boat could be heard outside the cave. The sound of the motors slowed down as the small Coast Guard boat entered the cave. Just as they hollered over to Lacey and Megan, Ben groaned and started to come out of his unconsciousness.

"What's goin' on?" he mumbled.

"You fell, busted your head open and Megan found a dead guy." Lacey said matter-of-factly. Ben put his hand to his head and felt the t-shirt tied to his face.

"A what? She found a dead guy?" he sat up quickly, and then swayed a bit, Lacey grabbed his arm.

"Yeah a dead guy, don't worry the Coast Guard is here now."

"Did you get the geocache?" he questioned.

"Yeah, Meg got it. No worries, buddy, just relax." A medic set his case down next to Ben and had him lay back down as he examined the wound.

"He's definitely gonna need some stitches and we'll have to have an eye doctor check out his eye. Can you walk kiddo?" The young Coast Guard medic asked Ben.

"Not sure," Ben responded. He tried to pull himself to his feet; slowly he stood up shakily grabbing both Lacey and the medic for balance. They moved him to the speed boat, where two other Coast Guard guys took him and sat him down.

A fourth Coast Guard Sailor popped up from the water channel in the middle of the cave and confirmed that indeed there was a body lodged between some rocks. Megan shook once again, having someone else confirm it somehow made it worse.

"We'll get you guys taken care of, let's load up those

kayaks." The first medic said to Lacey. "He can stay here with the corpse, until the other boat comes." He added as he motioned to the sailor climbing out of the water. Lacey helped push the kayaks onto a ledge at the back of the speed boat, then helped Megan climb aboard, and followed behind her.

The engines got louder as the boat slowly advanced through the cave. They were taking the back exit, which was exciting because Lacey really wanted to explore the whole thing. The cave grew darker the further they got from the front opening, and the ray of sunlight from the waterfall slowly disappeared behind them. The cave wound and bent around rocks, the water wasn't as choppy in the middle as it was near to the exits. Through the darkness the light of the Coast Guard boat illuminated the black stone walls. They were shiny and glossy, from the moist sea air. As they came out the back exit of the cave, they saw the towering cliffs of volcanic rock along the beach, they were magnificent, random patches of colorful vegetation grew in and around cracks in the volcanic stone, and despite there being little soil, the plants seemed to thrive.

Lacey turned from the beautiful view back to Ben, "How ya doin'?" she asked.

"Okay, I think. Hey did you guys open the geocache?"

"Not yet, you've got the key." Lacey reminded him.

"Oh yeah," Ben sunk his hand into his shorts pocket and removed the brass key, Megan held the metal box for him as he inserted the key and turned it quickly. As he lifted the lid, he saw another brass key and a note in a zip lock bag. "Here we go again." Ben said as he removed the contents of the box.

Lacey grabbed the bag from him while he looked at

the waypoint engraved on the key. Lacey then read the note out loud, "'*The Forbidden Isle*'…hmmm…that's all it says," she announced as she turned the note over, verifying there wasn't anything else written.

"I got the aerial map here," Ben pointed to the screen of his phone, "It's called Ni'ihau."

"Guess we'll be getting another flight." Megan said.

"Did you say, Ni'ihau?" one of the Coast Guard guys asked.

"Yeah, why?" Lacey questioned.

"That's a private island, you have to have permission to go, good luck," he replied.

"Dang, how's that gonna work?" Ben pondered.

"Let's get you stitched up and checked out, we'll make it work, it's not like we haven't gone into forbidden places before." Lacey winked at Ben and Megan then sat back in her seat and watched the coast line turn into a blur of greens, blacks and browns as the boat sped past.

❧

Ben stepped into the waiting room of the Emergency Room wearing a black eye patch which covered a large gauze bandage on his right eye. Running from his eyebrow and disappearing into his thick blonde hair was a long row of black stitches.

A young male doctor followed him and approached Lacey casually, "Okay, so slight concussion, luckily his eye and forehead will be okay, although he will most likely have a gnarly scar. He needs to rest, drink plenty of fluids, keep the wounds dry and continue to wear the eye patch for at least five days, seven would be even better." Ben rolled his good eye. "Also, he is on some pain medicine, here is a prescription, he'll need to take these every six to eight hours, with food. After a day or two he can just take them as needed for the headache, and of course, no operating heavy machinery while taking the meds." The doctor laughed at his own joke, and then quickly regained his composure when he realized it wasn't *that* funny. "Obviously I'm joking, he's too young to…well, you know," he waved his hand at them trying to move past the joke. "Anyways, any nausea, vomiting, extreme dizziness, then bring him back in." He handed the prescription to Lacey.

"Thank you, Doctor." Lacey nodded to Ben, making sure he was good to go; he responded with a nod and started walking to the door.

As they walked out of the automatic sliding doors of the Emergency Room, Ben turned to Lacey and asked, "What did Mom and Dad say?"

"They must be in the air, 'cause their phones went right to voicemail, don't worry I'm sure they're okay, and they'll be okay when they find out. Why don't we head to the hotel so you can rest."

"No, I really wanna get to the next cache, the island is really close. I looked more on my phone while I was waiting." Ben pleaded.

"Ben, you heard the doctor, you need to rest."

"I'm fine. I'll rest on the boat!"

"Boat?" Lacey and Megan both asked at the same time.

"Yeah, we'll take a boat; the cache looks like it's on the edge of the island. We can rent a boat, head to the cache, grab it and go, *easy peasy*."

"Seriously, you feel good enough to do that?" Lacey questioned.

"Yup." Ben responded immediately.

Ben lay back on the long seat that framed the interior of the boat. Lacey and Megan pushed off from the dock and slowly steered the boat around the other boats in the marina, it wouldn't be too long of a boat ride and they could just run onto the island, find the geocache and leave, no need to pay the owners of the island for a five minute trek along the beach, they thought.

As they exited the marina and accelerated past the jetty, they increased the speed of the boat, it sailed smoothly over the crystal blue ocean water. In the distance they could see Ni'ihau, for being a Hawaiian island they were surprised at how brown it looked, almost arid and desert like. They followed the waypoint on Ben's cellphone and made their way to the northern shoreline of the island. They slowly maneuvered around a large caldera that formed a perfect semi-circle in the water. As they floated toward the shore what seemed like hundreds of monk seals dove and splashed around them, they were enormous and playful, not at all scared of the intruders in their water.

To the side of the caldera was a small sandy beach, Lacey gently let the waves push them onto the sand, bow first. They all carefully climbed out of the boat onto the sparkling white sand underfoot. Pink colored Conch shells decorated the sparse beach, in the distance they saw only one palm tree.

Ben eyed his cellphone once again, "Okay looks like we need to be about two hundred feet to the right." he announced quietly. As they looked in the direction they needed to go they saw that the white sand quickly turned into black and brown rock, which jaggedly lined the cliffs on the side of the island.

Lacey began to walk in that direction, Ben and Megan followed. Megan stayed close to her brother, checking on him every so often to make sure he was okay. She was worried he might pass out at any moment from his injuries. He kept pace with his aunt though and continued to wave her off whenever she asked how he was. They quickly began to climb the rocks that lined the cliff, big boulders mixed with smooth lava rock. Ben swayed only a little as he stepped from rock to rock.

The cliff line was jagged and cracked, it was breathtaking, Lacey thought. She was always impressed with the places the Cache Master had taken them. As they moved over the stones more they saw that in the distance the cliff line had a large slender hole in it. Clear blue skies shone through creating an amazing vision. Ben quickly snapped a picture and sent it to his contact at United Cellular. He then checked the GPS once again, "I think the cache is by that hole," he announced. "This is called 'Keyhole Rock' by the way." he added.

"That's fitting." Lacey said as she moved closer to the cliff. They maneuvered over the large stones, using their hands and feet, and aiding Ben whenever he lost his balance, only being able to use one eye made his depth perception less than reliable.

They reached the edge of the cliff, which towered over them, and searched for the geocache along the baseline, not seeing it anywhere Lacey began to carefully climb the cliff wall, the bottom of the opening in the Keyhole Rock was only about ten feet off the ground. Just as she pulled herself to the base of the keyhole her hand brushed against a small metal case, "Found it!" she hollered. She didn't hear a response so she angled her head slightly to see why Ben and Megan hadn't gotten excited; as she did about a dozen Hawaiian men carrying machine guns caught her eye.

4

Lacey slowly and carefully climbed down the wall holding the geocache. As soon as her feet touched the ground two armed men, covered in tattoos, came to her, removed the geocache from her hand and then turned her around and bound her hands behind her back.

They spoke native Hawaiian as they walked Ben, Megan, and Lacey around the rocky cliffs and then up onto a dirt path. The land was even drier than they originally thought; few trees decorated the landscape and the grasses crackled under their feet. There were no roads or power lines, just barren land, a few scrawny deer darted across the path in front of them, it was as if they had arrived on a desert island, which was so strange considering how lush the other islands had been in Hawaii.

As they walked further and crested over a small hill, a tiny village could be seen in the distance. A few small, shack-like, homes surrounded a dusty barren road. Mules roamed in dry fenced pastures and dozens of bicycles leaned up against the modest houses. The armed men marched the trio into a small building, it had a dirt floor and a roof made of corrugated aluminum. The men pushed them onto the floor and had them sit while they used a hand radio to contact someone. Lacey tried to place the language but it sounded different from the Hawaiian she had heard spoken on their trip so far, maybe a different dialect, she decided.

Ben dropped his head to his knees and rested for a few moments.

"You okay?" Lacey asked.

"My head is pounding," he replied quietly. One of the men tapped him on the shoulder with his automatic weapon, forcing him to be quiet.

As they continued to sit on the floor several small children ran to the open doorway of the hut and poked their heads in, they analyzed the intruders and giggled at Ben, certainly the strange eye patch and crazy stitches decorating his forehead were amuzing. The huge burly men covered in intricate tattoos shooed the children away and gave a few some candy from their pockets. Megan immediately felt as if they couldn't be that mean, despite their appearance. After seeing them interact with the village youngsters she relaxed a bit and closed her eyes.

Minutes turned into an hour and finally there was a tap on the frame of the door, the men nodded and welcomed the visitor. A young teenage girl with long dark blonde hair stepped into the small shack. She nodded at the men and smiled sweetly, then turned to the intruders. "Hello, my name is Claudia, my family owns this island. We didn't have any registered visitors today, are you lost?" she asked, sounding amazingly professional for someone maybe fifteen years old, Lacey thought.

"No, we're sorry. We were geocaching and the waypoint led to the cliffs on the shoreline, we thought we would only be a few minutes so we didn't get permission, we actually didn't even know how to get permission." Lacey wiggled in her restraints as she spoke.

"Oh, are you referring to the geocache in the Keyhole Rock?" Claudia asked intently as she motioned for Megan to turn around and lift her hands. She gently and quickly untied her hands and asked her to sit back down. Then she moved to Ben and finally to Lacey, untying each one effortlessly. Megan wondered how many times Claudia had to untie intruders, and how awkward that must be to be such a young girl with so much power.

"Yes! Yes, the one in the keyhole, the men took it from us, but yes it was left by the Cache Master, we have been following all of his geocaches." Lacey said with relief.

"We know the 'Cache Master' well; he used to be a guest of my grandfather's. He would come to hunt and hang out with the villagers and helped plant trees along the island." Claudia responded. "Sorry about all this, the tribe here is very protective, outsiders are not welcome and they try their hardest to scare people away."

"Mission accomplished. What's with all the ink?" Ben laughed.

"What happened to you?" Claudia motioned to his face.

"A climbing accident trying to get to the cache before this one," Ben answered. Then he asked, "Do you have any water? I really need to take my medicine." Claudia stood and went to the doorway, her long flowered skirt drifted around her legs in the breeze. She said something in the foreign language and returned to the trio.

"It probably won't taste very good, we use rainwater on the island, it is filtered, but still, probably not what you are used to." She smiled apologetically.

"No worries and thank you!" Ben responded.

"What language are they speaking?" Lacey asked.

"Oh it's a Hawaiian dialect, from centuries ago, very different from what you will hear on the big islands." Claudia answered. She seemed so grown up and mature for her age. A man brought in a small cup of water and handed it to Claudia; she responded gratefully then passed the water to Ben. Lacey reached in her shorts pocket and pulled a prescription bottle out, then opened it and handed a large pill to Ben. He broke it in half and swallowed the pieces quickly. "So, I'll need to check with my grandfather and uncle, about any fines, but I'll talk to them about you not understanding the rules for coming onto the island." Claudia pulled a cell phone from a pocket in her skirt and proceeded to make the call.

"Please tell them we are so sorry for trespassing." Lacey interjected. Claudia nodded and then stepped outside the hut.

"Fines?" Megan asked.

"I guess." Lacey shook her head in frustration. "Sorry you guys, I guess we should have made an appointment and asked permission or something, how do you even go about doing that though?"

"No clue. Did you see these guys though? I'll be glad to pay a fine as long as they don't burn us at the stake." Ben said as he relaxed against the plywood wall of the hut.

A moment later Claudia stepped back inside, "Good news," she beamed, "No fines, however my grandfather and uncle would like to meet you. They actually helped Mr. Morgan...er...uh, The Cache Master plan this whole thing you're doing." She motioned for the group to stand and follow her. Along the backside of the hut were several mountain bikes, Claudia pointed to them as she climbed on one, pulling her skirt to the side. "Can you ride?" she asked Ben.

"Yeah, I think I'm okay." He responded. They each climbed on a mountain bike and followed Claudia as she pedaled quickly up the dirt path leading out of the small village. They rode for about five minutes before coming to a large fenced area, it looked like a compound. A heavy framed wrought iron gate seemed to be the only access point. Claudia pushed the heavy gate open then motioned for the others to ride their bikes through. She closed the gate behind them then proceeded up the driveway. In the distance a large home could be seen with a few smaller houses off to the right and left.

"This is the main house." Claudia informed them. They all dismounted the bicycles and followed Claudia in the large wooden door of the house. It wasn't grand or intimidating, very modestly decorated, with more natural elements like potted palm trees and drift wood. They all walked into a large den area that had floor to ceiling windows and overlooked an amazing view of the ocean. The crystal blue waters danced and sparkled in the distance. Claudia motioned for them to sit on a couch against one of the walls while she went to retrieve her grandfather and uncle. A moment later she returned with the two men who were dressed in identical tan shorts and Hawaiian shirts, both donned wide brimmed hats that reminded Ben of Indiana Jones.

"So, you guys are tracking Mr. Morgan's geocaches, huh?" One of the men asked as he sat in a chair across from the group. The other man sat in a recliner a few feet away.

"Yes, sir." Lacey replied. Then added, "We are so sorry about not getting permission, we really thought we would only be a few minutes and had no intention of going any further on the island." She made big puppy dog, apologetic eyes at the older men.

"That's okay, it is complicated to get out here, but we like it that way, we don't like anyone bothering the natives here on the island, we're just trying to protect their way of life." Lacey shook her head, confused. "If you own the island, why do you let them live here still?" she asked.

"Well, they were here first!" the other man answered as he chuckled. Then he got more serious, "Just because our Great Grandmother purchased the land didn't give her the right to push the natives out of their homes, this has been ingrained in all of us. We were gifted this land by our family because they knew we wouldn't ruin the land, we would just live on it and enjoy it without turning it into something that our relatives never envisioned." He paused, "That is one of the reasons Mr. Morgan enjoyed coming here so much. First, it is, of course, a nice change from Alaska," he and his brother laughed loudly, "but also because we maintained the true heritage of the island, we try very hard to keep the natives happy and their lives private."

"Huh," Lacey nodded trying to understand why they were being told this.

The other older man interrupted her thoughts and added, "Mr. Morgan always believed that whoever finished his scavenger hunt would know what he wanted to happen to his land in Alaska. By making you see all of the different things you have seen, you'll have your answer just when you need it." He sighed sadly for a moment, "Poor guy, he couldn't trust his own sons to follow through with his wishes for that land, that's why he turned it over to fate…or…well, you three, I guess." He cleared his throat thinking of something he was holding back, "He was a good man, he never knew that his land would be filled with such controversy, after his youngest son died he knew he couldn't trust his oldest, after he was diagnosed with terminal cancer he came down here to visit for what would be his last time. We all sat down and came up with an idea of how to find the perfect benefactor. Now you are following through with that. Let me ask," he paused and looked at Ben, "Did that happen to you at Pirate's Cave?" He looked mischievously at his brother.

"Yes, sir." Ben answered. "I fell when I was trying to get to the geocache."

"I told you!" the man hollered at his brother, "I told you that was too dangerous!" he shook his head at his brother. "Glad you're okay." The other man made an apologetic smile at Ben. Lacey and Megan giggled at the man's outburst. "Well, we probably shouldn't keep you. Thank you for coming to speak with us, Mr. Morgan was a dear friend; we hope you will honor him when the time comes. Remember one thing for me, though…well for Mr. Morgan; all of the places he has taken you have purpose, each is important to your journey. And even when it feels as though this task is too complicated or too hard, never forget to enjoy that journey."

The men stood as did Claudia, "Come," she motioned to them, "Let's get your geocache."

As they rode the bikes back into the small village, Ben saw everything from a different point of view, these people weren't scary, they were peaceful, living off the land, using rainwater to survive. They didn't have power, or cars or plumbing, and one thing that he noticed about each and every one of them, they were all smiling.

As they climbed off the bikes once again, Ben felt a wave of dizziness overcome him, he swayed for a moment and then got his balance. The heat, combined with the bike riding was not agreeing with his concussion, he thought. He followed Lacey and Megan as they walked and spoke more with Claudia. She approached a tall man; his tattoos covered his entire back and crested over his shoulders, running down onto his chest and arms. She asked him something in their native language; he shook his head and disappeared into the small house he had been standing in front of. He returned with the small metal box Lacey had recovered from Keyhole Rock. Ben watched as he turned and spoke to an older man who had approached slowly. Ben studied the tattoo covering the man, it appeared to be a dragon or serpent of some sort, rising out of a volcano, its body made of fire. As Ben looked around at the other men, who were waiting to see what was inside the geocache, he noticed that they all had the same intricate design decorating their flesh.

Ben anxiously dug in his pocket to retrieve the key; lifting it carefully in his hand he inserted it into the lock on the geocache. It turned smoothly and the lid popped open. Ben reached inside and collected a small slip of paper and another brass key, "Guess we're not done yet." He said to Megan and Lacey. He unfolded the paper and read the note the Cache Master had left for them.

"*The sword in the stone.*'" Ben looked at the note once

more, "That doesn't make sense, huh…well; I guess we'll find out." He shoved the key and the note into his pocket, and then asked Claudia if she could ask the natives for their permission to take a picture of them with his cell phone. They all agreed and formed a group; the children bobbed happily and were eager to see the images on Ben's cell phone afterward. He sat and showed them all the pictures he had from their journey, the bears eating salmon in Alaska, Iditarod, the dog sledding, Pirate's Cave, he had so many pictures, it was nice going through them and remembering where they had been.

Claudia joined the group, sitting in between Ben and Megan, as the children quieted down Ben finally had the opportunity to ask, "What is with all the tattoos, these guys are covered in ink!" he said as he motioned at all the men. Claudia shrugged then called the men over to their group. She then stood and began asking the same man who had delivered the geocache something in their native language. The man grabbed his friend's arm and turned him around, pointing to the design stretching across his broad frame, as he spoke Claudia relayed what he was saying,

"He says this is the Pana'ewa, or umm…giant lizard, that Pelehonuamea, the goddess of the volcanos, asked her uncle, Lono-Makua - the keeper of fire, to protect the sea of fire along with Ke-o-ahi-kama-kaua, which means something like: the spirit of lava fountains. That spirit brought Ke-ua-ake-po - the spirit of the rain of fire, to help him. They protect the volcano from evil to preserve the circle of life." Claudia said something else to the man, and then thanked him.

"The *kua-mua- whata*?" Lacey asked Ben. He laughed at her then recovered when he noticed Claudia and Megan both glaring at them. Lacey quickly replied,

"Sorry, that wasn't funny...sorta." She looked at Ben mischievously.

The men walked away, as they did the older man approached them slowly, and looked over to Ben, as the older man turned to speak privately to the other man Ben noticed that he had the exact same tattoo, the dragon was made of fire but instead of red flaming eyes, this dragon had bright blue flaming eyes. Ben stared at the man's wrinkled and hunched back taking it all in, and then asked, "Why is the old man's tattoo different?"

"I'm not sure, but he is the tribe leader, maybe it has a different significance?" she stood and walked to the men speaking privately, then interrupted them and asked something. Nodding in gratitude she thanked them then headed back to the group. "I don't know what everything in their language means; sorry...all he said was something like he is 'the keeper.'" She shrugged her shoulders apologetically. Ben's mouth hung open in shock, had she just used those words...*The Keeper*? He closed his mouth quickly, deciding to keep his shock to himself.

The group said goodbye and began walking back up the dirt path that led to the beach where they had been captured earlier that day. As they walked Ben's vision became a little blurry, he saw black and white dots in his peripheral vision and he was stumbling more than usual. Suddenly, out of the corner of his eye he saw the tall body of The Keeper, he appeared to be floating next to Ben, his long black cloak blew in the warm breeze. As Ben stumbled once again The Keeper's long fingered hand appeared from within his cloak and gently grabbed Ben's arm bringing him balance once again. Ben smiled and thinking he was hallucinating he shook his head trying to clear his eyes, as he did, The Keeper disappeared.

"You doing okay?" Lacey asked him. He nodded and

continued walking. They weaved around the winding trail that cut through the cliffs and down to the beach; the white sand glistened, looking as though it were covered in crystal glitter. The sight was so beautiful it took them all a second to notice that their boat was gone.

5

"Please tell me you bought the insurance." Ben asked Lacey.

"Uh…nope, everyone always says the insurance is a rip off." Lacey shook her head in frustration.

"Unless your boat gets ripped off!" Megan joked. Ben and Lacey looked at her and rolled their eyes.

"Well let's see if we can find Claudia, maybe she can help?" Lacey said as she turned in the sand and headed back toward the cliffs. They walked all the way back to the village and tried to communicate with some of the natives to get a hold of Claudia, or one of the older men that owned the island.

A helicopter hovered next to the small village, and then carefully landed in the dry weeds of a pasture, the farm animals all ran, fearing the intrusion. Ben, Megan, and Lacey ducked while they covered their eyes and ran through the tornado of dust and debris being blown everywhere from the propellers. They climbed in and buckled up. One of the older men handed Lacey a headset, she slipped it on and thanked him for his help.

"Did you forget to anchor the boat?" he asked.

Lacey blushed then responded, "Yeah, I'm not exactly a boater." He chuckled and then slowly lifted the helicopter off the ground.

As they flew over the island they could see just how arid and dry the land really was, it was so different and sparse than any of the other islands they had seen.

"Why is it so dry here?" Megan asked.

"The big island steals all the rain," the pilot replied. Megan nodded her head acting like she understood exactly what he was talking about.

As they floated over the beaches everyone looked in different directions for the boat, about a mile off shore to the north Ben saw it floating in the current. "There!" he hollered trying to get everyone's attention. The pilot sped over the glistening waters toward the boat.

"Okay, we'll have to lower you down using the rope and harness." he informed them.

"What?" Lacey shouted.

"How else would we do it?" he asked expectantly.

"Oh yeah, okay," Lacey took a big breath and looked to Ben; he was very pale and seemed to be overwhelmed with fear, "I'll go first." Lacey insisted, she climbed to the back of the chopper and with Claudia's help got into a harness that attached to a long thick nylon rope that was wound around a large spool which would electronically lower them down. Claudia instructed her to sit on the edge of the chopper and then slowly push off. She explained that the rope was secure and that the pulley system would lower her very slowly into the boat. Lacey dangled her legs out the door of the chopper. They were hovering above the boat about seventy-five feet up. She took a deep breath then pushed off the edge gently. The harness became tight around her hips and chest, and then Claudia started the electronic spool, Lacey began to drop slowly, she swung about a little as the chopper adjusted to the wind, but for the most part the drop was easy and smooth.

Finally, her tip toes touched the floor of the speed boat. She let out a huge breath, which she decided she must have been holding the entire time during her descent. She unhooked the harness and stepped out of it, then gave a thumbs-up to Claudia who was leaning out the opening of the side of the chopper. Very quickly the rope began to rise up above her head.

Ben shakily stood next to the open doorway in the chopper, even though there was water below him, fear had crawled up his entire body, his anxiety grew with every second. Claudia tightened the harness one last time then instructed him to sit on the edge as well. Reluctantly, he sat down and then while closing his eyes he slipped out the edge of the chopper. The rope and harness became taut, just as Claudia had described. He kept his eyes closed and tried to focus on his breathing and controlling the nausea in his gut. The combination of the pain medicine and now the over whelming fear wasn't being received well by his stomach. As he was being lowered the warm breeze tickled his face and for a moment he felt a smile come to his mouth. With his eyes closed this really wasn't that bad. Suddenly he felt a hand on his leg; he yelped in fear threw his legs out and kicked someone very hard. He instantly opened his eyes apologetically.

"Ben, it's okay!" Lacey said, she was doubled over in pain, but continued to steady him down into the boat. He had kicked her right in the gut. She grimaced in pain, but didn't say anything to him.

"Sorry, I...I..."

"It's okay," she interrupted him. She unhooked his harness, and then gave another thumbs-up to Claudia. Once again the rope disappeared above their heads.

Megan eagerly stepped into the harness and sat on the edge of the chopper. She slipped off the edge and screamed with pure delight as she was being lowered. Suddenly, something didn't feel right though, and there was a strange sensation on her back from the harness. She wiggled trying to figure out what it was, just as she did a strong wind whipped her around and she began spinning in circles. The chopper above her lurched, as it lurched again the back of the harness snapped, and she fell backwards.

Ben and Lacey screamed as they watched everything happen above them. Luckily it appeared that Megan had grabbed onto the nylon rope just in time, she was hanging upside down, still sixty feet over the water, spinning in circles. She screamed and cried loudly as she closed her eyes in sheer panic. The chopper began to bob and weave; another strong wind blew by and pushed the chopper even more. The pilot tried to correct it, but with each breeze it jolted the rope and flipped Megan around violently.

"I've gotta get out of here!" the pilot called to Claudia, "The wind is too strong, I've got to get above it, or we're going down!" he quickly pulled up on the hand control and the helicopter lifted quickly, once again jolting the upside down Megan. Again she shrieked in panic. Her hands were burning as she held onto the rope, she could feel it cutting into her palms, and she could feel the increasing sweat on her skin make her grip even weaker. As she sailed through the air she opened her eyes. She continued to spin relentlessly. Claudia had stopped the pulley system, from lowering Megan, but now with the chopper in motion the system wouldn't work to pull her back up.

Tears ran down Megan's forehead as she spun uncontrollably upside down. She began to wonder if she should just let go and fall into the ocean, surely it was deep enough to not cause any injuries. She couldn't be totally positive though, so she continued to hang on with all her might.

Ben and Lacey followed the helicopter as quickly as they could; it was heading back toward the island. Watching Megan hang upside down at least two-hundred feet in the air was terrifying. Lacey tried to push the boat to go faster, just in case Megan fell into the water, but at full throttle they were still lagging very far behind.

As the helicopter came over the beach, it reared up even more to avoid the cliffs, Megan saw the rocky ledges coming right for her and closed her eyes tight as she prepared to hit the cliff at full speed, luckily just in time she flew right over them, and was only feet off the ground. The chopper slowed as it gained stability over the land. Suddenly Megan felt movement in the rope, she was being pulled back up, she continued to hold onto the rope as tightly as she could. The tears continued to pour down her forehead as uncontrolled sobs poured out of her lungs. Finally, she felt a hand on her hand, Claudia was leaning out of the edge of the chopper grabbing onto her. She quickly pulled her inside. Megan fell to the floor of the and cried a little more before regaining her composure. The pilot looked back and apologized

~ 43 ~

profusely, and then slowly brought the helicopter down to the ground.

As the propellers stopped Claudia began inspecting the harness, "I am so sorry Megan; I don't know what happened." She eyed one of the carabineers; then realized that when Lacey took it off Ben she must have unclipped the wrong clasp. "I should have checked this, I'm so sorry," she showed Megan what the problem was, and then hugged her verifying she was okay. Lacey and Ben ran up the dirt path toward the chopper and pulled Megan up in a big hug as soon as they arrived. She buried her head in Lacey's arms, and then started laughing.

"O-M-G!" she wailed. "Can you believe that?"

"I am so glad you're okay!" Lacey nearly screamed at her.

"I can't wait to tell my friends about that, please, please tell me you got a pic." she asked Ben. Ben was shocked at her behavior, but figured she was *kinda* crazy anyways.

"Sorry, I was so freaked, I didn't," he replied.

Megan looked to Claudia then asked, "Any way we could do that again?" Claudia's jaw dropped, she couldn't even think of a response.

With all the drama from the day before and the lecture she had received the prior night from Ben and Megan's parents, Lacey was feeling overwhelmed and thoroughly exhausted. She understood that danger was part of this game, and that going to all these forbidden and exotic locations would bring an element of the unknown, the unexpected, and of course what to some would seem like the unachievable. Lacey knew that they had to carry on though, she knew the importance of their mission; at least she was beginning to think she did.

Lacey, Trent, Megan, and Ben were climbing onto trail horses; they had rented them for the day to travel into the Haleakalā Volcano, on the island of Maui. Lacey and Trent had packed day packs, with snacks and plenty of water; they would be descending into the volcano's dormant crater in search of the waypoint which would hopefully explain the clue of *'the sword in the stone'*.

The Halemauu trail wound for miles through burnt red cinder cones and ebony black lava flows, volcanic glass decorated the landscape just as shrubs would in any forest. The peaks and valleys of the volcano were incredible, one moment they could see an endless view of the ocean, the next they would be in a deep depression, with cliff like walls surrounding them.

The horses did well, in spite of the hot temperatures. They seldom spooked or tripped, despite the rocky trail floor beneath their hooves. As the group descended deeper into the crater, Lacey recounted the events of the last few days to Trent; he listened intently, as only an endeared boyfriend would. Ben had noticed that she had brightened as soon as she saw him the night before. He realized she was just as worried about Trent as they were about their parents. He audibly breathed a sigh of relief once again accepting that everyone was safe.

As time passed Ben captured pictures of various parts of the crater and trail, as they crept lower and lower he began to notice an odd plant. The plant had sword like gray leaves that grew up in a circle around a large stock that was covered in dark purple colored flowers that resembled small sunflowers. It was so odd, he thought, that this plant could grow right out of the dry volcanic cinder. Ben searched the internet until he found a matching plant.

"I think I know what the clue means!" he called out to everyone. "These plants are called 'Silversword' they only grow here, and somehow survive all of the weird weather the crater creates." He continued to read as everyone halted their horses. "They were becoming extinct, but now are starting to come back since they are being protected, and they only go to seed once, then they die. Well, no wonder they were becoming extinct." He tapped his phone's screen to check the waypoint once again to see how far off they were. "Okay we have 20°43'10.44" North and 156°11'51.35" West…" he paused while his phone gave the remaining distance, "We're only a few hundred feet away from the waypoint!" He nudged his horse forward and began leading the group in the direction his GPS pointed.

The rough lava floors of the trail cracked under the horse's hooves. With every sound Ben clinched a little. He noticed the wind picking up, a rough dirt and sand like dust swirled around them and the temperature seemed to drop severely. Ben shivered a bit, as he did he heard someone say, "Caution."

He looked back to Megan, "What did you say?" he asked.

Megan looked at him with confusion, "Nothing, why?"

"Huh, I thought I heard someone say something." He turned his attention back to his GPS unit; they were quickly approaching their destination. With that encouragement he tapped the horses belly with his foot and held on as his horse began to trot and then gallop. He wailed with delight as he sailed through the red and brown slopes of the crater. As he reached the waypoint he dismounted and grabbed the horse's reigns carefully leading it through the crunchy earth off the trail.

Ben approached the skeleton of an old Silversword plant, the waypoint was correct so he looked around the base of the dead plant's leaves. *It must have gone to seed*, he rationalized. As he got closer to the plant his horse began to twitch and fight the advancement, Ben yanked on the reigns trying to force the horse closer. He didn't want to let go and have it wander off, but he also didn't want it to spook and drag him off either. He turned to soothe it and it reared up on its hind legs, throwing its head and neighing loudly. Trent, Lacey, and Megan approached from behind and dismounted as well. Their horses began reacting to Ben's horse, throwing their heads and rearing up on their hind legs, they accidently bumped into each other and irritated one another even more.

As Ben was trying to gain control of his horse he heard an eerie crunching and cracking sound, suddenly the brittle ground below him and the horse began to crack and crumble, gravity was taking over and Ben was falling through the ground. Lacey, Megan, and Trent gasped and surged toward them as they saw the horse and Ben struggle to move. The force was too much and the ground collapsed too quickly, within seconds a huge vent opened up to an underground lava tube and both the horse and Ben disappeared.

6

Ben's head pounded, his throat felt tight and dry, a film of dirt covered his nostrils. Breathing felt almost impossible, the tightness in his chest circled around like a massive rubber band cutting off his ability to inhale deeply. He wiggled his fingers and toes then moved his hands and feet, everything seemed to be working properly, there was just a dull ache everywhere.

The horse next to him seemed to gain awareness at the same time as Ben; it rolled and wrestled its way up onto its shaky legs. Debris fell from the large animals back and as it shook a cloud of dust wafted off into the dark cavern that had swallowed them up.

Ben pushed some rocks and dirt off of his chest and hips and managed to pull his aching body onto his feet. Small slivers of light cut through the dusty space and illuminated dots on the ground, like lasers. As the ground had fallen the debris blocked the potential exit overhead,

Ben's throat got tighter as he realized he was trapped. Cautiously he raised his hand and moved slowly toward the spooked beast in front of him. The horse had calmed even though it had just fallen through the earth. "You must have known, huh, bud?" Ben soothed the animal as he grabbed the tangled reigns. The horse's body went still and the rippling muscles appeared to calm under Ben's touch.

Ben stepped into one of the rays of light; he wiggled his cell phone out of his shorts pocket and lifted it toward the ceiling of the cavern. The ground had given way so quickly he wasn't sure how far they had fallen, or how far they were under the surface. As he lifted his phone it vibrated in his hand, Lacey was calling. He pulled it to his ear quickly.

"Are you okay?" she yelled. Ben responded through the scratchy and failing reception,

"Yeah, yeah, we're okay. I'm hurting, but okay. Do you see any way out from up there? Everything is caved in down here."

"No, there is just a small crater, the dirt and rocks completely covered where you fell through. Are there any tunnels or anything down there?" she asked.

"Hang on a sec'," Ben lifted his cell phone away from his head and using the screen to illuminate the space he peered through the dusty haze, turning in a circle he paused when he saw that there was indeed a tunnel that broke off to the right. "There's a tunnel down here, I have no clue where it goes; my phone is my only light. I don't know how long I'll have reception." His belly churned with anxiety.

"Can you use your GPS map down there to tell me which direction you'll be going, we can follow above ground and check in. Maybe we'll find a skylight or something to get you out of there." Lacey was turning around looking into the distance trying to see anything that looked like a possible escape route for Ben.

"Just a sec'," Ben responded again. He tapped his phone's screen until the GPS app appeared then walked toward the tunnel. A line formed on the screen with a small arrow, and the letters 'SW'. "Okay, you there?" he paused thinking he'd lost reception.

"Yeah, yeah, does it work?" Lacey asked, rushed.

"For now it does shows I'm going South West."

"Okay, for now take that tunnel, we'll walk above ground and see if we can make contact or find an exit point. I'm worried if we try to dig you out more rocks and debris could collapse in on you." Lacey analyzed the crater in the ground in front of her, next to the crater she saw a familiar box resting on its side. "Hey good news, I found the geocache!" The earth crunched under her feet as she delicately and deliberately took one careful step at a time, fearing she may also fall through the surface. She kneeled and scooped the warm metal box into her hand, wiping the dust off of it as she returned to Trent and Megan.

"Oh, good. Okay I'm gonna go, I don't want my phone to die, I'll start walking and I'll try to call in a few minutes to see if I still have reception." Ben hung up the phone before Lacey could say anything else. He rubbed the palm of his hand against the soft, smooth fur of the horse's muzzle, "I don't even know your name, boy." He whispered. The horse's rubbery lips nibbled on Ben's thumb. "Let's call you 'Freaky', 'cause you freak out and make the ground cave in." He paused and continued to feel the satin-like fur of the horse's face. "Maybe you knew it was dangerous? Did you, boy, did ya?" Ben raised his phone up, lighting up the horse's face, as it reflected off the horse's eyes shivers ran up Ben's arm and crawled like spiders up his neck. His chest grew tight once more as he stared into bright crystal blue eyes. "I don't remember you having blue eyes before," Ben mumbled. A deep breathe filled Ben's lungs and somehow soothed his anxious stomach. He turned and with the low glow of his cell phone began to make his way down the dark tunnel.

With every step the ground crunched below his and the horse's feet. It was more stable than the earth above; the lava that had cooled and created this tube was more solid than the vent they originally fell through. This brought a comfort and fear to Ben. It was more stable, yes, they most likely wouldn't fall through and into an even lower cavern, but if it was too solid, how would they get out?

Ben felt the air cool as they advanced into the tunnel; they appeared to be staying level and after a few minutes of walking by the glow of his phone his uncovered eye was able to see much more clearly. The dust had settled and the tightness in Ben's chest had disappeared. He stopped his progression through the underground space for a moment and checked his phone's service bars. There was one teeny tiny bar where usually three or four bars stood. He pressed the icon and called Lacey's phone.

"Good, you still have service." Lacey said quickly, then added, "I'm gonna stomp on the ground, let's see if you can hear it. Suddenly the horse's ears perked up, Ben listened more intently and heard the faintest of booms from the earth somewhere above him. As he listened he saw small flakes of dirt and stone fall from the ceiling above a few feet in the distance.

"Yes! I can just barely hear you, but I think Freaky can hear you even better." he explained.

"Freaky?" Lacey paused.

"Oh, the horse, I'm calling him Freaky." Ben explained. "Okay I'm gonna go so I still have a battery for the light." He hung up and continued to move down the dark tunnel. The expanse of the tunnel was reassuring to Ben, his shoulders seemed to relax as he evaluated the size and height, this was different than the caves in Oregon, much wider by at least ten feet and the height varied by ten to fifteen feet, he thought. Also the walls in this cave were smoother, as if the lava cooled more quickly and didn't form into individual stones first.

Freaky's ears lifted at attention once again, Ben forced himself to hold his breath as he listened, again a few feet ahead he heard a tapping on the ceiling above him, he quickly texted his aunt a smiley face, figuring that texting might use less of the battery than calling. He heard the tapping once more, verification that she had received the text message, he thought. Once again he carefully walked down the tunnel; his head was pounding with the beat of his heart, as if the itchy eye patch and stitches weren't enough of a reminder of his injuries. He blinked his good eye a few times, trying to force the pain away. Nothing seemed to help, even the medicine the doctor had given him only helped the first hour after he would take it. Trying to distract himself he spoke softly to Freaky, explaining the geocaching trip and all the crazy things that had happened to them, he found himself pausing waiting for a response and then remembering that of course he wasn't going to get one. Freaky followed closely behind, his head low except when they would hear the tapping, only then would he lift his head and perk his ears forward.

After another twenty minutes of monologue Ben realized that he hadn't heard the tapping in quite some time, Freaky didn't seem to hear anything either, he sent his aunt a text, and got a warning that he had no service, "Great," he mumbled. Then his phone vibrated and a low battery warning came on the screen, "Seriously?!" Ben groaned. The thought of having no light source sent a chill down Ben's spine. The tunnel was so completely dark that without the dim glow of his cell phone he would be in total blackness, not just darkness, but blackness. His head pounded in a quicker succession, sending shooting pains into his eyes and behind his ears. He realized he had to calm down, his pulse was spiking as his anxiety grew.

"Let's move faster, 'eh Freaky?" he said to the animal. Freaky followed Ben's quickened pace, again never lifting his head, hearing absolutely nothing. As the tunnel continued to stretch before them, with no sign of light in the distance Ben became frantic, his phone vibrated in his hand once more, surely having the backlight on constantly was eating his battery like sharks on a boat-size steak. He checked the screen, the warning indicating he had only five percent of his battery life left. He picked up his pace, the sound of the crunching lava rock beneath their feet being the only sound he heard.

Another minute later his phone vibrated in his hand and then everything went completely black. Freaky stopped walking as Ben frantically tried to turn his phone on again. With no success he slid his hand around his shorts until he found his pocket then let the phone drop in. "What are we gonna do now?" he asked no one. Again his head pounded harder and faster in his skull, the sound behind his ears was almost as painful as the pounding itself. He closed his eyes, as if closing them would change his surroundings giving him an opportunity to think. His throat grew tight as his reality set in, he could feel the lump growing below his voice box, and heard his own breathing become quick and shallow.

Dark places didn't usually scare Ben, but being in complete blackness in a cave was something different entirely. What else was in the cave, he quickly thought back trying to remember if he had seen any spiders, had there been any snakes? Bats? A long list of creepy crawling animals and insects started flowing through his brain, an image of a human size bright red centipede with stingers, covered in mucus flashed in his mind, and then he thought of all the other things, were their bones? Were there bodies? Moisture pricked his eyes as his fear took over, and then he felt the furry, silky muzzle of Freaky on his cheek.

Freaky moved, frightening Ben as he thought he might get stepped on, but instead the reign in Ben's hand pulled him forward. "Freaky, wait!" Ben tugged hard on the reigns. "I can't see anything!" his voice cracked as the words escaped. The horse paused for a moment and then took a few more steps forward, if Ben didn't move he would soon be dragged. He stepped forward with the horse, at first Freaky would take two or three steps and wait for Ben to match him, finally as Ben calmed a bit, Freaky continued forward at a slow pace as Ben took blind step after blind step forward.

The overpowering blackness was suffocating, every few feet Ben was sure something had touched his face or grabbed onto his foot, it was as if he were in a different cave entirely than the one he had previously been in. Suddenly, instead of smooth lava stone walls, Ben's mind was telling him these walls were made of slimy, green, stinky filth. Instead of the floor being covered with crunchy lava rock, Ben was sure that he was walking on bones, and although he didn't recall seeing any spiders or bats earlier, images of countless movies flashed in his mind and he began swatting at his back and neck, rubbing his hands anxiously through his hair and around his throat as he envisioned himself covered in creepy crawly highly venomous tarantulas and vampire bats.

"*Trust.*" He heard the word whispered. Was he imagining it, he wondered? He realized it was the same soft, raspy voice he had heard earlier on the trail that had said 'caution.' Ben dropped his head to his chest and scrunched his eyes as he inhaled the cool crisp air of the tunnel. He continued taking blind step after blind step, *just one foot in front of the other;* he started repeating in his mind. The words started to flow in rhythm with the pounding pain behind his ears. It created a strange melody in his head, which he tried to distract his anxious thoughts with.

He maintained a good pace, although every step was an obstacle, real or imagined, Ben couldn't tell. He was sure the crunching under his feet sounded different than it had when he had his phone to guide him, *were these bones? Am I walking on thousands of skeletons, their dry bones breaking and crumbling below me?* Ben tried to dismiss the thought from his mind, he shook his head and felt a fluid run down the tip of his nose and the side of his face, he just knew it had to be blood. His wound must have opened up when the cave in happened, he thought. He rubbed the liquid on his face, *yes, this definitely feels like blood*, and it felt like a lot of blood, Ben decided.

His throat tightened more as images of zombies crawling and climbing down the tunnel behind him filled his mind. He saw their rotten flesh and black eyes, their sharp teeth as they sniffed the smell of his dripping blood. Suddenly, he felt a hand or something around his throat, it was squeezing so tightly he couldn't breathe. He paused and Freaky stopped beside him. Ben gasped for air, he pushed his own hand to his throat and felt nothing, but from inside something was restricting his breathing. His hand moved down to his chest, where the panting of his lungs lifted his ribs under his fingers. *I'm being strangled, but by what? A ghost?* The image flashed in his eyes, a horribly scary ghost, with its long fingered hands wrapped tightly around Ben's throat. Then Ben remembered caving in Oregon, the sound of the CO_2 alarm rang in his ears, as if it were right here in this cave now. Ben threw his hands to his ears trying to block out the invading noise, *that's what's happening*, his mind screamed out, *I'm running out of oxygen! I can't breathe!* The liquid again dripped down his nose and from around his eye patch, in the blackness Ben could only imagine his wound pouring out, spurting red explosions of blood. Instantly Ben felt dizzy, he fell to the floor of the cave and wiped the liquid off his face. He looked around in the blackness, sure that something was right beside him, he couldn't see anything as he swung his head from side to side in a psychotic panic, but he knew-he just knew he was luring most likely *zombies and vampires and ghosts and tarantulas and vampire bats, and snakes, oh no! I forgot about the snakes! And the blood, I'm bleeding to death, this is pouring now!* He felt his shirt, it too was soaking wet, *have I bled that much?! And the air, there isn't oxygen, yes I'm sure of it - I can't breathe*, he choked as he tried to inhale, but his dizziness was too great, *it's the blood, I've lost too much blood!* He thought. The darkness seemed to become thick and smothering around him and with his last raspy breathe he sighed "I'm sorry." to no one.

7

Lacey, Megan, and Trent began to panic as they tapped on the ground and got no response. Lacey tried calling Ben's cell phone over and over and it went to voicemail every time. As they advanced over the lava field in the direction they thought the tunnel would go, they ended up going up a small rim and walking on the loose volcanic rock.

"We must have gotten way off course," Trent announced. "Maybe we should head back downhill and see if we come to anything."

"Okay," Lacey and Megan said in unison. They gripped their horse's reigns and led them down the rim and back into the desolate crater of the volcano. As they proceeded over the vast crater they saw the tops of trees far in the distance, down below the crater rim on the side they were approaching. They continued to walk toward the tree tops, hoping that maybe the tunnel let out just below the rim on the other side. The rocks got larger as they topped the edge of the rim and began carefully climbing down the side of the crater. On this edge of the volcano was a thick rainforest. The canopy of the trees looked like a dense carpet from up above. As they descended they heard the faint whiney of a horse.

"Listen!" Lacey commanded as she held her hand in the air. Everyone including the horses grew instantly silent, holding their breath. Again the sound of a horse whinnying whispered through the air. "I think that's Ben's horse!" Lacey moved quicker down the rocks, only slowing to allow her horse to carefully maneuver alongside her.

When they reached the bottom of the rainforest and stepped onto the rich brown soil the sound of the horse got louder. They followed their ears and rounded the base of the volcano's crater. Tucked within the large stones and boulders were all sorts of cave openings, some very tiny, others were a decent size. Lacey was tempted to go into each one to try to track down Ben, but focused on following the sound of the horse instead. As the neighing got louder, Lacey's shoulders relaxed a little, and her stomach, which had been in knots, loosened. Finally the group rounded a small outcropping of large boulders and to the side was a large cave entrance, where Ben's horse stood. Lacey's heart felt as though it may explode when she realized the horse was all alone. "Ben!" she screamed, the sound so loud and deafening that Megan covered her ears. There was no response; the only sound that could be heard past her echoes was the snorting and stomping of Ben's horse in the cave entrance.

Trent approached the horse and looked it over, he caressed its muzzle and asked "Where's Ben? Huh? Where'd he go?" As if he would get a verbal response.

Instead the horse turned around and trotted back into the cave. Trent gave Lacey the reigns to his horse, turned his cell phone on, to provide light and quickly entered the cave after the horse. He followed the tail end of the animal as it rounded corners and trotted ahead. The cave provided an easy trail, the floor was covered in crunchy lava rock, but besides focusing on not rolling an ankle there were no other obstacles. Trent inhaled deeply allowing the refreshing crisp air to fill his lungs. After walking for what felt like hours in the hot and dusty crater of the volcano, the coolness was very welcome.

A minute later Trent slowed as he saw the horse standing still. He moved his cell phone all around the cave and saw Ben on the floor in a heap. He was drenched, covered in sweat, and deathly pale. Trent looked him over and felt his legs and arms, trying to feel for broken bones or any indication of what may have happened to him. "Ben?" He shook his leg. "Ben?" Trent kneeled behind Ben's lifeless body and scooped him up under his armpits. Just as he did Ben woke and let out a huge, terrifying scream. He kicked and tried rolling out of Trent's arms.

"No! No! Let go of me, please!" he wailed.

Trent let go of him and interrupted Ben's pleas, "Ben, Ben it's me, Trent." He turned the cell phone on his face, illuminating it, then shone it back onto Ben, who was sweating profusely and in tears. "Hey, what happened? Are you okay? Did you get hurt?" Ben stood up and shook his shoulders, then wiped some liquid off his head, he drew his hand into the light and suddenly his body went limp with relief as he saw that the fluid covering his face was just sweat. Ben then lifted his shirt into the light and laughed when he saw that it too was only saturated with sweat.

A deep, loud sigh of relief, parted Ben's lips, and then laughter took over, "I don't know what happened, I thought I was bleeding, I couldn't see anything, my phone died and I had absolutely no light. All the sudden I felt like I couldn't breathe, I thought I was dying, suffocating." He took a deep breath allowing his chest to puff out as he inhaled. "It's weird, seems like the air is fine now."

"Ben in total darkness, not knowing where you were, you probably had a bit of an anxiety attack, those can make you feel like you can't breathe sometimes." Trent reached out and grabbed his arm, "Let's go, the end of the tunnel is about thirty feet up ahead."

Ben turned bright red. "Are you serious? Wow I feel like a loser!" he moaned.

"Hey, it's fine, no one needs to know. Besides anyone would have panicked being in a pitch black tunnel that they didn't know where they were going, no worries, buddy." The sound of the crunching lava rocks underfoot intensified as Ben's eagerness increased. "You don't always have to be the hero, Ben," Trent added. "Sometimes, the real heroes are the people who admit when they are human. Does that make sense?"

"What do you mean?" Ben panted, as he was almost jogging.

"I mean, real heroes are normal people who find themselves in situations where they overcome stuff, sometimes we can overcome stuff, and sometimes we can't. But real heroes know that they are never losers, as long as they try." Trent paused waiting to see if Ben understood.

"Oh, yeah that makes sense," Ben stopped for a second then added, "So as long as I keep trying, I'm a hero?"

"Always keep trying, but don't do it to be a *hero*, do it because you want to, no matter what anyone else thinks." Trent clarified.

"Okay." Ben continued jogging and almost yelped with excitement as he made it out of the tunnel. He lunged onto Freaky's neck and gave him a big embrace, burying his face in his soft fur.

Lacey ran over and hugged Ben, then Megan joined in, "What happened?" she asked. Ben looked at Trent for a minute then answered, "My phone died and I had no light, I kinda panicked I guess." He smiled at Trent.

Then Trent added, "He was only about thirty feet from the opening of the cave, must have walked a long time in the dark to get that far after your phone died, pretty brave, my man." Trent smiled and nodded acknowledging Ben's braveness by telling the truth of what had happened to him.

"Thanks," Ben blushed. "Aunt Lacey do you have my medicine, my head is killing me." Lacey dug in the pack on her horse, then handed Ben a pill and a water bottle.

"We've got to be careful with you, Ben, the doctor said you need to be resting, and this hasn't exactly been leisurely for you." She frowned; disappointment in herself covered her face.

"I'm fine, just tired, and sore, now where's the geocache?" Ben tried to change the subject, the last thing he wanted was to end up cooped up in his hotel with his parents while Megan, Lacey, and Trent did all the crazy stuff. Lacey reached into her pack one more time and pulled out a small black box that matched all the others.

"Right here, you still have the key?" she handed it to Ben as he dug in his shorts pocket. He lifted the small brass key up and theatrically moved his arm around as if he were some sort of magician then slipped it into the lock.

He paused before lifting the lid, "And this ladies and gentlemen will be our final clue!" he sarcastically announced in a cheesy voice, as he lifted the lid then removed another brass key from inside the box he then added, "Or… maybe not!" Everyone laughed together and secretly hoped it would be their last clue; there was just no way of knowing until the Cache Master said it was over.

❧ ❧

"I think we've done more flying on this trip then even in Alaska," Megan said as she grabbed her small day pack out from under her seat.

"We're getting close," Trent replied as the group quickly exited the small airplane. "Seems like it takes a lot longer when I'm not doing the flying though," he added. Lacey grabbed his arm affectionately.

Ben rolled his good eye to Megan, and she giggled and blushed, "You look so funny in that eye patch."

"Shut up…you're just jealous you don't get to wear one," he joked.

"Uhhhmmmmm, nope." Megan responded. They made their way out of the small airport and onto a windy street. The air was moist and easy to breathe here; it was so different than the dry, desolate volcano they had been on previously.

"So, it looks like we're going to the jungle," Lacey announced. "Let's figure out how we're gonna get there."

"I vote for an air conditioned vehicle," Ben replied.

Lacey looked at Ben, his skin was a grayish yellow hue, the bruises on his face were healing nicely, but he still looked rather ill, "You feeling okay, buddy?" she eyed him skeptically.

"Yeah, my head is pounding, but yeah, I'm good" he looked away from her, worried she might make him sit this one out or something.

She gently put her hand to his shoulder, "Let me know if you need your medicine, or a break, we can relax for a day, you know."

"I just wanna get done, and then we can take a break." He looked at her hand and raised his good eyebrow.

She instantly removed her hand then said, "Sorry your highness, I forget I'm not cool enough to touch your shoulder." Lacey stuck her tongue out to an un-amused Ben.

❧

The palm trees sailed by quickly in a rush of greens and browns, as the Volkswagen Baja Beetle cruised up the narrow road that bordered the jungle. As the foliage became more dense, Ben's chest grew tighter and his heart beat escalated. He knew they were getting close, the Kamakoa Preserve was just ahead, which meant the next geocache was as well.

Lacey studied the GPS map on her phone; she looked out the window and saw a small turnoff and a dirt trail that appeared to head into the dense jungle. "Pull off up there," she told Trent, he looked at her expectantly, "Eh-hem…please." She added. Trent smiled and slowed the car to a stop on the side of the road.

"Okay guys," he announced to Ben and Megan.

He lifted the driver's seat forward as they both anxiously climbed out of the cramped Beetle. As soon as he closed the door he felt Megan's small fist on his bicep.

"Slug Bug!" she yelled, and then laughed.

Trent rolled his eyes. "You've called it like ten times, it's the *same* car!" Trent complained.

Megan laughed as she recalled pounding his arm every time she had seen the reflection of the Beetle in a store front window or when they stopped for fuel. "This is a different time of me seeing it, don't hate...I didn't make up the rules, and it's not *my* fault *you* don't understand the game and are *losing*." She laughed louder. Trent sighed and gave up, then rubbed his sore bicep.

"She's little, but she can really hit." He whined to Lacey. Lacey shook her head, ignoring him, then began hiking up the dirt path that led into the jungle. The path was overgrown with ferns and palms, coconuts littered the jungle floor along the edges of the soft soil.

Loud birds cawed, announcing the intruders into the jungle, other animals screeched and called, Ben jumped every time, the sound echoed in his head, making the pounding fiercer. He scrunched his good eye closed as he tried to push the pain out. Nothing seemed to be working, even with the medicine the pain seemed to be getting worse, maybe he *should* sit out for a day and relax, he thought. As the group approached a deep ravine, this thought seemed like an even better idea. His stomach clenched as he looked over the edge. Jagged rocks and random trees popped out of the cliff walls that dropped over one hundred feet to a small rocky creek bed below. Just to the left the trail turned and an old rope bridge stretched and sagged across the empty air between the two cliffs. "Great," Ben groaned to himself. As he looked at the creek bed below again a wave of dizziness blurred his vision. He loudly sucked in a huge breath of air, trying to calm his senses.

"You gonna be okay?" Lacey asked.

Ben looked to her almost panicked, "Yep, I'll be fine, let's hope this bridge can hold us. Rock, Paper, Scissors for who goes first?" he raised his hands up.

"Nope, I think Trent will go first." Lacey announced.

Trent swung his head around to her with a panicked and confused look, his eyes scrunched and he shook his head, "Uh...I like Ben's idea," Trent said. Lacey's lips hardened into a thin line, and then she motioned to Ben's face using just her eyes. Trent looked at Ben sheepishly, acknowledging his bandages and eye mask. "Okay, how 'bout just Lacey and I will do Rock, Paper, Scissors?" He smiled mischievously at Lacey.

"Oh fine, you big baby, I'll go first!" she hollered.

"Oh no, no..." Trent raised his hands in a joking manner making obnoxious gestures, "We're playing," he sarcastically demanded.

Lacey shook her head and rolled her eyes, "Fine," an irritated smile spread across her face as she drew her hands up and formed a fist over her other palm, "One-Two-Three," she pumped her fist then kept it in 'rock' formation, "Haha," she smirked, "Rock crushes scissors!"

Trent frowned then released a heavy sigh as he turned toward the sagging rope bridge, only to see Megan half way across already, "Hey!" he called to her; she turned quickly, standing on a small weathered piece of wood being held by two braided ropes. Her hands gently gripped the ropes at her sides.

"What?" she called back to the group.

"I was supposed to go first!" Trent yelled across the ravine.

"I wasn't included in that conversation," Megan announced in an annoyed tone. "So, I decided while you whined I would go." She turned and continued to step carefully from board to board over the decrepit bridge.

Ben laughed to himself, then stopped when Lacey glared at him, "What?" Ben asked raising his shoulders, "That's just *soooo* Megan, ya know." Lacey nodded in agreement, Megan was feisty that was for sure.

Lacey stepped up to the bridge next, "I'll go after her." She told Ben and Trent. She stepped onto the first piece of decaying wood; it creaked and bowed a little under her weight. She inhaled deeply trying to calm herself. As her hands slid over the hand ropes she could feel the bridge bowing and flexing as it adjusted to Megan moving over it. The swaying made Lacey dizzy, as did looking down below her, which was never a good idea. She scolded herself immediately for being so stupid.

Carefully she moved her foot to the next plank of wood, and then took two more steps out over the ravine. She looked back to Ben whose uncovered eye was huge with fear for his aunt. Lacey turned back around and saw that Megan was just a few feet from the other cliff wall. She sighed in relief knowing that Megan was almost on solid ground again. She decided to increase her speed to catch up to her niece. Once again, Lacey moved her foot to another plank, then one after the other she advanced. The bridge creaked and swayed again, suddenly a scream cut through the silence. Lacey jumped in a panic and looked across the bridge. Megan was struggling in Henry's grasp as she tried to fight him off to get free.

"Henry!" Lacey shrieked. "Leave her alone! How did you get out of jail?" Lacey moved quicker across the bridge, she was standing almost in the middle of the bridge, the old rope and wood planks sagged below her, but anger was driving her to move faster.

"I posted bail," Henry called out. "Did you forget that I can track your cell phones?" he coughed as he let out a hoarse laugh. Quickly he tied Megan's hands and feet and had her sit on the ground, and then he moved closer to the bridge, he drew a large hunting knife out of his belt and placed it on one of the ropes that anchored the bridge to each cliff. "I'll give you instructions on your phone, you call the cops and she's dead, you understand?" he hollered as he viciously sawed the rope with his knife. The rope began swinging back and forth; Lacey grasped the hand ropes as tightly as she could. Suddenly, the foot planks fell to the side as Henry's knife cut clear through the rope. Lacey screamed louder, her feet tried to grasp the planks, but couldn't. She hung on to the hand ropes and then felt half of her body being pulled back and forth again as the ropes moved furiously. She looked through her angry tears over to Henry again; he was sawing the hand rope now.

"Don't do this Henry!" Trent yelled across the ravine.

"Shut up, Lover Boy!" Henry growled. His knife made a clean cut through the hand rope and suddenly there was nothing holding Lacey on that side, her body fell slightly, and instantly she moved her falling arm to the other hand rope. She tried to begin moving back towards Ben and Trent, sliding her hands as quickly as she could. The old rope was becoming red as the blood from her raw hands slid down the fibers, tearing and stinging deep into her flesh. She moaned in pain, and then felt that the rope holding her was being wiggled and swayed, she looked past her extended and burning shoulders over to Henry, he was now sawing this rope, the only rope she had left.

The tears stung her eyes as she called out to Megan, "We'll come get you, don't tell him anything! It's okay Megan, we'll…" she sucked in more air as the tears poured down her face, "We'll get you!" Just as the words escaped her lips a loud snapping noise echoed in the ravine. And as if she were moving in slow motion Lacey was falling. She hung onto the rope as tightly as she could; she turned to the direction she was falling, back toward the cliff that Ben and Trent were standing on. She saw the rocky walls coming toward her, again as if in slow motion, she didn't know what to do. The wind blew through her hair, a sign that she was indeed moving faster than her brain would allow her to process. As the rope spun and slipped through her hands the rock wall came closer and closer in sheer panic she closed her eyes and screamed.

8

Megan's wrists stung from the rope cutting into them, her mouth was parched and dry, the bandana Henry had gagged her with smelled of sweat, with every breath her stomach churned with nausea. The back of the rented SUV was at least clean, she wiggled her ankles and was reminded that Henry had restrained her by tying them to one of the seat belt latch clips in the rear of the vehicle. Although fear was building in her belly she couldn't help but feel optimistic for some reason, perhaps it was that she considered Henry to be less than intelligent, or maybe just that she knew somehow this couldn't be the end for her, whatever it was she wasn't allowing panic to overcome her, ironically her apathetic attitude was driving Henry insane. He had expected her to be terrified and fighting, when she climbed into the rear of the SUV and allowed him to tie her up he was dumbfounded. It wasn't that she planned on being so agreeable, it was more a tactic she had learned from school, when a bully would pester her if she ignored it and acted like it didn't bother her the bully would usually give up and leave her alone. The same was true for Henry she assumed, he was just a bully, and she wouldn't allow him the pleasure of knowing that she was scared, she could play this game; she had to.

Megan felt the car slow and then turn right, she had no clue where she was, she couldn't be too far away considering they were on a tiny island, her body lifted and rolled slightly as the car went over a speed bump, then slowed to a stop. She squinted her eyes as the tailgate lifted and warm bright sunlight poured in.

"A-2," Megan mumbled through her gag, the bold large letters were painted on the side of a garage door that Henry was unlocking. He knelt and pulled on a rope that lifted the rolling door, in either direction Megan saw many other garage doors, lining the cinder block building, she realized that they were at a storage unit of some sort.

Henry walked over and pulled on the rope binding her hands, she carefully slid off the back of the SUV and hopped into the storage unit, as she did the rope around her ankles slapped the cement floor. The cool air was a welcoming feeling for Megan; she looked at the empty space wondering what they were doing here. The walls were made of two-by-four wood studs, with old water damage sheetrock nailed haphazardly to each stud. Mold and mildew decorated the stained sheetrock in large circular blooms of green and brown where the water had stayed the longest. Megan crinkled her nose at the thought of being in a mold infested building. As they reached the left far corner Henry shoved her to the ground. She looked at the sheetrock and wood studs before resting her head against them, in this corner she was safe, if not from Henry, at least from the mold, she rationalized.

"You're gonna stay here, when they get me the money then I'll get you out, don't try anything stupid, little girl," Henry barked. Megan restrained herself from rolling her eyes, she hated being called *little girl,* she instead chose the more appropriate response and nodded her head slowly in agreement with him. As soon as he stood and turned away she couldn't help herself though and she rolled her eyes and shook her head, *what a moron,* she thought. She followed Henry with her eyes as he reached to the top of the rollup door and grabbed the rope; he stepped out of the unit and slowly lowered the door, as the last little bit of light disappeared Megan's stomach churned with anxiety. She blinked a few times trying to adjust her eyes in the pitch black room. As she did, she saw tiny beams of light shining through the wall on the opposite side of storage unit. The beams cut through the darkness like tiny lasers, Megan stared at the beams of light trying to formulate a plan; nothing was coming to mind, so she gave in to her drooping eyelids and drifted to sleep on the cold cement floor.

Lacey closed her eyes tightly as dirt and debris fell onto her face, forty feet above her Ben and Trent were pulling the rope on which she hung. As it cut through the earth on the side of the ravine all sorts of stuff became loosened and gave in to gravity. She moved her feet up the rocky wall as they continued to pull, this helped in two ways, one: Ben and Trent didn't have to lift dead weight, and two: her body wasn't being dragged along the jagged rock wall, bumping into every rock, limb, or shrub that protruded from the surface.

Lacey spat some dirt from her lips and shook her head back and forth in an attempt to clear the dirt and filth from her face. Inch by inch she felt a little safer and her body seemed to relax, although the burn in her shoulders was quickly spreading through her ribs and chest. Bright red blood dripped slowly down from her palms, staining the old rope that dug into her flesh. Her hands throbbed in pain from the tearing in her skin and the pain of holding her grip for so long, soon she would be to the top, she tried to convince herself, but then what? How would they get to the other side, and even if they did what would they do, get the geocache and continue to play this ridiculous and dangerous game with Henry? As she shook her head no, answering her own question, the top of the cliff came into view as well as Ben and Trent's feet.

Her legs kicked and clamored as she tried to pull herself over the edge and onto solid ground, as she shimmied on her belly she bellowed as a sigh of relief echoed out of her lungs. Immediately, Lacey's hands were pulled into her stomach and chest, she cradled her torn flesh as she evaluated her wounds. Ben knelt next to her and gently poured cold water onto the wounds, trying to clean the worn rope chunks, blood, and dirt from her palms.

"What do you wanna do?" Ben asked Lacey. His own head was pounding fiercely, from helping pull his aunt up the cliff.

"Not sure. We have to get Megan back; we need to get rid of Henry once and for all, how on earth did he get out of jail?" Lacey rubbed her palms on her shirt trying to clear more debris.

"I think there is only one way we're getting rid of that guy." Trent interrupted.

Ben nodded then replied, "Yeah, we're gonna have to kill him." Lacey and Trent both looked at Ben in astonishment.

"Uh, I was gonna say give him the money, but um…well…I guess *killing* him works too." Trent raised his eyebrows, as his eyes widened in a *'what on earth?'* expression.

Ben stared at them both a moment then gave his justification, "If we don't he's never gonna stop, we'll be giving him the Cache Master's land, do you guys really wanna do that?"

"I just want us to be safe, I mean look at us." Lacey looked at her hands and gestured to Ben's bandage and eye patch, "Not to mention Megan, I mean, I don't think that Henry will kill her, if he was that type he would have killed us all a long time ago. We just have to get her back and end this all."

"Okay, so how do we get to the next cache, with the bridge out? If we wanna end this let's get the cache and head to the next one, Henry will be tracking our phones, he'll follow us for sure." Ben looked over the embankment to the ravine below. Nausea slowly swirled in his gut, his throat tightened and instantly hairs and sweat prickled up on the back of his neck. He instinctively rubbed the back of his neck, almost trying to wipe the fear away, it wasn't working.

"I can't climb down that rope, if that's what you're thinking Ben." Lacey said as she buried her hands in her shirt, trying to soothe the burning prickly feeling radiating from her skin.

Ben laughed, as he smirked at his aunt, "You really think I would want to climb down this side and *up* the other side, have you *met me?*" He shook his head in disbelief that she would even fathom such an idea, then pulled his phone from his shorts pocket, after a few taps on his screen he flipped it over so Lacey and Trent could look. "I think this could work, we just have to see what *this* is." He pointed to a large brown box shaped item that appeared to be suspended in the air by two ropes or chains.

The picture on his phone was blurry from being zoomed in so much, so no one could really be certain, "And where exactly is this?" Lacey questioned.

"If the satellite imagery is accurate and recent, this thing should be about a mile up the ravine through the jungle. Trent and Lacey both looked in the direction Ben's hand was extended. With all trees, shrubs, weeds, vines, and masses of other vegetation, visibility was about ten feet.

"Wait, you expect us to bushwhack a mile through that mess?" Lacey's mouth and eyes stayed wide, "Really Ben, *really*?"

"Really, really," Ben imitated her voice for effect.

A huge sigh of discomfort escaped Lacey's mouth, "Okay, let's just make this is fast as we can, we gotta get to Megan and I wanna be able to give Henry *something* so he'll leave us alone." She stood gently and rubbed her shoulders and arms then her lower back, her hands continued to burn and sting, but the water had helped and somehow knowing this was all just beginning made it easier to deal with the pain, there was really no other choice.

The thick jungle was relentless, vines grabbed onto Ben's feet as he plodded through, the fallen leaves and debris had created a soft cushion underfoot, which made walking even more difficult, the varying unevenness of the earth and random holes that were covered by vegetation made bushwhacking not only frustrating but dangerous. As the group walked on, lifting their legs over fallen trees and branches, pushing palms out of the way and screaming randomly while swatting almost invisible large spider webs from their faces and bodies, it felt as though they would never reach their destination. Ben continued to eye his phone, watching it painfully slowly reduce how many feet they had left to travel. Finally after two hours- which felt more like five-they arrived at a small trail. The trail continued up the edge of the ravine, it was overgrown and not worn as much as the original trail they had been on. Ben watched his feet as he convinced his body to continue just one step at a time. He noticed about an hour earlier that he was having a hard time seeing the screen of his cellphone clearly, thinking he was just tired and needed rest he continued on, not mentioning anything to Lacey or Trent, the last thing he wanted to do was make them think he was a whiner, especially when he was the one who recommended bushwhacking in the first place.

Trent threw his arms in front of him and hollered, "There it is!" Sure enough in the distance were two large metal cables supporting a makeshift wood trolley. The trolley was maybe three feet long and a foot wide; it rested about fifteen feet out over the ravine on top of the cables.

"What is it?" Ben asked, as he increased his speed to catch up to his aunt and Trent.

"Looks like a cable trolley, people use these to get across and haul loads of stuff across, a little less work to build and maintain something like this than a rope bridge." Trent explained.

"So how we gonna get it?" Lacey asked, her hand motioning that it was far out of their reach over the ravine.

"Hmmm, let's look for a long branch or something," Trent rambled as he stepped back into the jungle, a moment later the jungle canopy began to move.

Lacey called to Trent, "You okay?" The tree tops and vines continued to jostle in the distance.

"Yep, just trying to knock this thin tree over!" he called back. Suddenly a cracking sound echoed in the ravine and the tree came falling down through the dense brush. A second later Trent was hauling it out of the jungle. It was bushy at the top, with a long, slender gray trunk that stretched about fifteen feet before the foliage erupted into a mess of green and yellow leaves.

Trent carefully threw it over the edge, continuing to hold on to the end, he moved it out slowly foot by foot until finally the bushy end made contact with the trolley. Lifting it carefully he rested the bushy leaves on the side of the trolley and began pulling the long tree back towards him. The trolley screeched as it moved back, the wheels of the pulley system it rested on were rusted from being in the moist jungle climate so long. As Trent made his final tug the trolley halted at the edge of the cliff.

Trent knelt down on one knee as he looked over the trolley and the cables; he pushed down on it for a moment gauging how strong it was then looked at Lacey and Ben. "I think it's safe," he beamed.

Lacey eyed him suspiciously, "You go first, then," she said matter-of-factly. Trent nodded then carefully climbed onto the trolley. It was a flat surface with a one inch lip on all sides creating a big rectangle, the only problem that Ben could see was there was really nothing to hold on to. Trent adjusted his body so he was kneeling on his knees facing toward the ravine, then he leaned forward and grasped the metal cables, carefully he pulled the trolley toward his hands, it wobbled a bit and moved forward. Ben held his breath as he watched Trent inch his way across the ravine, one arm pull at a time. After what seemed like an eternity Trent had made it to the other side, once he was off and on solid ground again he grasped the trolley and with all his might he pushed it hard. The trolley flew back over the cables almost all the way to the other side of the ravine.

Ben grabbed the long tree once again and raised it over the ravine. He made contact with the trolley and just as Trent had done he pulled it to the edge, knowing that Lacey couldn't manipulate the tree with her damaged hands Ben motioned for her to go next.

"You sure?" she questioned.

Ben nodded, "Yup, just be careful as you pull yourself across, wanna wrap your hands in my shirt?" She looked to her torn skin then nodded appreciatively. Ben carefully pulled his sweaty t-shirt over his head, making sure not to hit his stitches or eye patch. He handed it to Lacey after she had adjusted herself in the trolley. Lacey stretched the shirt between her hands then placed them on the cables and began to painfully pull herself out over the ravine. Ben heard her small sounds of pain with every grasp of the cables; he knew her hands were burning and most likely her shoulders, chest, and neck from hanging on to the rope bridge only hours earlier. As she crossed the ravine he squinted to focus on her more, noticing she was getting very blurry in the distance, he rubbed his good eye to try to clear the blur, it didn't work. As he waited he decided to sit and rest a moment with his eye closed, perhaps that was all needed, he thought.

Shortly after resting on the jungle floor he heard his aunt scream, he jumped at first and then realized she was screaming with elation that she had made it across. Ben grasped the tree in his hands again as he waited for

Trent to push the trolley back, within a few seconds the trolley came to a halt at about the same place it had the first time. Ben extended the tree out and moved the trolley back to the edge once more. His head pounded loudly in his ears as he climbed onto the platform. As his heart anxiously pumped faster his wounds paid the price, aching and throbbing took over his skull.

"Don't look down," he said to himself quietly. Ben reached out and focused on the two cables that stretched like power lines across the ravine in front of him, he grabbed each one with sweaty, shaky palms and began to pull. The trolley shook and wavered below him. His stomach tightened in nauseous knots. He focused again on only the cables, his blurry vision was actually proving to be useful, he thought, he couldn't really see the ground below him, only the thick, burnt-red rusted cables which he held onto for dear life. With each movement and screech of the trolley's wheels he cringed, waiting, holding onto the cables a little tighter, just in case the trolley fell. When it didn't he could feel the knots in his shoulders and neck release the slightest bit, then as he moved his hands forward and pulled again the pounding fear in his head and tight anxiety in his neck and shoulders would return. As if the physical challenge of pulling himself across a hundred-foot wide ravine on a trolley weren't enough, the emotional challenge seemed almost worse. Finally as he arrived at the other edge, he let out a huge sigh, tears pricked his eyes as Trent reached for his hands. He gulped loudly, forcing the knot of relieved stress back down out of his throat.

"Good work, Ben!" Lacey gently hugged his shaking frame then handed him back his blood stained and now rust covered shirt, he motioned for Trent to turn around and quickly tossed it into his hiking pack.

"You'll need it on the way back," Ben explained as he frowned apologetically at Lacey. She sighed as she looked forlornly at her torn hands then peered up at Ben's torn and stitched face, she quickly swallowed her self-pity realizing how lucky she was to have come out of such a terrifying experience with only torn hands. Ben looked down the pathway that led from the trolley bridge; then pulled his phone out of his pocket.

"Okay," he said, "We don't have that far now that we already bushwhacked; check it out, only another mile into the jungle up that way!" Ben paused then sighed, "You brought the extra phone battery this time right Aunt Lacey?"

Lacey nodded then motioned once again for Trent to turn around, "Your battery running out again?" she asked as she handed the small black square to Ben.

"Yeah, probably just from having the GPS on the entire time, must eat it up," Ben complained. He handed the drained battery back to Lacey as he popped the new one into the phone. "You guys ready?" he asked. Lacey and Trent nodded in unison, "Let's get this cache and get Meg back," Ben said as he began marching on the soft dirt path underfoot.

The jungle passed by quickly along the pathway as they carried on following the directions of the GPS. Finally they came to a small rocky cliff edge; below the edge was the jungle canopy creating what appeared to be a lumpy carpet of green and yellow.

"So the GPS says to continue going straight, but the path veers off along the cliff edge, it looks like it stretches for miles up the mountain ridge," Ben pointed off into the distance. "What do we do, we can't climb down this cliff, can we?" he looked over the edge and shivers ran up his sweaty arms and back.

"Looks like it's too sheer of a cliff wall, there aren't really any handholds." Trent said as he gazed over the edge as well. "I wonder though..." he then sat on the edge of the cliff and kicked his leg toward the closest tree. His shoes caught one of the top bushy branches, "This is the same type of tree we used at the trolley; they are very bendy." Trent explained as he pulled the tree's canopy closer to the cliff ledge.

"Bendy?" Ben questioned. Trent wrapped his hands around some of the branches then carefully slid off the cliff. The tree swayed for a moment and then finally began leaning in the direction Trent's legs hung. The thin gray wood bent slowly and lowered Trent to the ground, as his feet made contact with the soft jungle floor below he let go of the tree and it quickly popped back up into an upright position again.

"*Seriously?*" Ben looked to Lacey.

"Worth a shot, I guess" she mumbled as she sat on the edge and carefully swung her leg out to the tree as Trent had, as she pulled it toward the cliff she called to Ben, "Get down here, you do this turn, I don't know if your legs are long enough to pull it toward you or not." Ben reluctantly sat beside her and peeked through the lush leaves down to Trent.

Trent caught his gaze and called up, "I'm right here buddy; I'll catch you when you get close enough, no worries, man."

Ben inhaled deeply then grasped the branches, "Okay, one...two...three." He continued to sit there, his good eye closed. Lacey looked at him expectantly, then once again he counted, "Okay, one...two...three..." he sat petrified once again. Ben began once more, he swallowed loudly then, "One...two..." Lacey saw his hands tighten on the leaves, as quickly as she could she used the back of her hands and pushed his hips, he sailed off the ledge of the cliff and slowly fell through the air as the tree bent under his weight. Screaming in terror for the entire two seconds until Trent grabbed his ankles and lowered him to the ground.

Ben looked up to Lacey, "Thank you, I guess," he called.

"Anytime, buddy." Lacey called back as she once again swung her leg out and grabbed the tree's canopy, she gently grasped the branches with her tender hands and slipped off the cliff, within a second Trent caught her as the tree popped back up maintaining its original posture. "We good?" she asked. Trent and Ben nodded, then turned and followed the GPS again.

Within five minutes they came to a large tree that was different from all the others. Its trunk was at least four feet wide; it rose out of the jungle floor for perhaps sixty feet. Along its lengthy base were what appeared to be at least fifty thick vines, upon further inspection they realized they weren't vines, but rather the roots of another tree that was growing on top of the large tree. This tree had grown out of the large tree and its roots stretched down the trunk and into the ground.

"Absolutely incredible," Lacey sighed as she looked at it more carefully.

"Its gotta be here, the Cache Master would have wanted us to see this," Ben beamed. Then Trent called over, "It's over here!" Lacey and Ben jogged to the other side of the tree. At the base of the large tree was a large opening, it created a small cave within the trunk. The roots of the tree which grew out of it crisscrossed over the opening creating a lattice like pattern. Deep inside the hole they could see the dust covered metal box. Trent looked at Ben and Lacey then shoved his hand in between the roots and into the hole, in a split second the look of excitement on his face turned to sheer terror he screamed at the top of his lungs and tried to pull his hand out of the hole. It wouldn't budge, he jumped and wiggled and couldn't get free. Ben and Lacey jumped and tried to figure out what was going on, they stared at Trent's trapped arm and watched blood pour down to his elbow.

9

Megan sighed in the darkness, not sure where she was or what she should do; she focused on the little dots on the floor. She followed the glittering light beams back to their source, they were coming from holes in the sheetrock between this storage unit and the one next to it, and then it occurred to her, there was sunlight in the next unit, the door must be open! She let out a muffled scream, as she started rolling over to the wall the lights were coming from. Her bindings dug into her skin as she made contact with the cement, but she easily pushed the pain to the back of her mind.

Once she got to the wall she pivoted on her back so her feet faced the little dots of light. She raised her bound legs and then kicked at the sheetrock. With the first kick the paper coating cracked into a big spider web pattern, *great security*, she laughed to herself. Again she kicked the same spot on the sheetrock, this time the clay and paper dented under her feet. Finally, she kicked one more time and her feet went through the wall.

The space between the two-by-four studs was only about twenty inches. Plenty of room for Megan to get through, but she wondered why no one had come to her aid. Her feet were literally hanging out the other side of the wall. Instead of giving up she decided to kick again to enlarge the hole, perhaps someone had just left the door to the storage room open, she rationalized. She kicked again and again; chunks of sheetrock fell to the floor coating her in a white powdery substance. Once she had created a large enough hole she pulled her feet back to her chest and rolled to her side. She shimmied and wiggled using her bound hands and shoulders to lift her body onto her feet. Once she did, she knelt down and pushed her head through the hole she created, at that moment she realized her mistake.

Trent screamed in pain, and thrashed his arm back and forth.

"What is it?" Lacey yelled at him, while grabbing his other shoulder.

"I don't know an animal I think, it's got my hand, it's gonna bite it off!" The panic in Trent's voice was evident. Ben came running toward the tree with a thick, long stick; he pushed it into the hole in the tree as hard as he could. It immediately hit something. He pulled it back again and with all his might shoved it in even harder, suddenly when it felt as though he had met resistance, the stick kept on moving forward and the animal in the tree cave let out a blood curdling squeal. As Trent ripped his hand from the hole bright red blood splattered Lacey's face. The stick was thrashing around so fiercely Ben had to let go. It moved freely in the latticed roots that covered almost the entire entrance to the cave, the painful squealing that echoed inside the hole was excruciating to listen to, although it was a better sound than Trent's relentless screaming, Ben thought.

They all backed away from the thrashing stick while Lacey washed and bandaged Trent's mangled hand using his shirt. Skin and flesh hung from the large bite wounds, "Was that a wild boar?" Trent asked through his panting.

"That's my guess," Lacey replied as she made the final wrap around his wrist. Already the tan fabric was turning a dark shade of brown as the wrapped layers absorbed the blood. "We're gonna have to get you to the hospital, a pig's mouth can't be sanitary." Lacey turned to head back the direction that they came.

"Where ya going?" Trent hollered. "We gotta get the geocache!"

"Are you sticking your hand in there again?" Lacey asked wide eyed as she pointed to the thrashing stick inside the hole.

"Uh…no, I guess not," Trent conceded.

They both looked to Ben, "Don't look at me!" Ben said raising his arms defensively. Just as he did the stick slumped in the hole, there was one final squealing cry and then all became eerily quiet. "Oh no, I think I killed it," Ben ran toward the tree.

"Don't you dare stick your hand in there!" Lacey yelled as she ran to block Ben from the hole.

"I'm not gonna, I'm just gonna move the stick to see if it is dead or not!" Ben retorted, pushing Lacey to the side. He grabbed onto the stick and tried moving it between the roots once again, it would barely budge. He tugged on it and it slowly came out, covered in blood and a coarse black hair. "I killed it." Ben slumped to the ground ashamed.

"You saved Trent's hand, Ben; it's okay." Lacey patted his shoulder. Then crawled over to the tree, she slowly pushed her hand through the tangled roots, as it brushed something warm and wet she drew her arm quickly out. She looked wide eyed with fear to Trent and Ben, swallowed loudly then with all her courage she slowly inserted her hand once again. The warmth of the hog's body didn't scare her this time; its course hairs tickled her wrist as she forced her hand farther into the cave. Once moving past the hog's back she angled her arm down and searched with her fingertips for the geocache. Her fingers grazed the top of the cool metal box; she smiled eagerly then stretched even further to lift it up. Once it was in her hand, she moved quickly trying to get the geocache out of the hole. Just as her arm rubbed the pigs body again, the pig spasmed and squealed. Lacey ripped her arm from the hole as fast as she could, a loud scream escaped her lips as she fell backward onto the ground, her arms flailing and legs kicking, as if the hog had jumped out and was attacking her.

"Holy cow, it's still alive!" She rolled quickly to her side trying to get her balance and lift herself back up, she panted as she tried to contain her fear. "Oh crud." Lacey looked down to her shorts. Ben began laughing loudly; Trent turned pink but didn't say a word as he stared at the wet spot on her shorts. "This didn't happen! Okay guys? Okay?!" Lacey warned. She huffed then threw the geocache to Ben.

"It's okay Lacey, as soon as we get to the car we can stop and pick up some diapers for you." he laughed.

"I thought it was gonna attack me, you would have peed your pants too!" she huffed, folding her arms tightly across her chest, and then lowered her hands trying in vain to cover her shorts. "Well let's get outta here, we've got to find Megan, get Trent to a hospital, and pick me up another pair of shorts, not *a diaper* Ben!" Lacey began walking back the direction they came in. Ben hurried to her side and showed her his cell phone; he had just entered the coordinates from the latest key.

"What does that look like to you?" he asked. Lacey peered at the phone then tapped the screen to zoom the picture out a bit.

"Looks like a ship wreck, search online and see what you can find."

"I will in a minute, I had an idea for finding Megan, I can look on my family map and see the places her cell phone has been within the last twenty-four hours, that should take us to her, as long as Henry has kept her cell on." Ben manipulated the screen on his phone a bit more, and then called out "Bingo!" The map on the screen showed Megan's phone represented in pink and Ben's phone represented in blue. The two icons matched up perfectly, and then the pink icon moved away from the blue one, registering long pauses at three different locations. "I say we go to the first location on the map, then the second if we can't find her, and so on," Ben concluded.

❧❧

Megan held her breath as her eyes adjusted to the light. Immediately she realized that the beams of light were not coming from sunshine, instead they were coming from several big lamps that hung over dozens of large cages. This wasn't as much of a concern to her as the cage that was lying on its side below her. Wood shavings had spread over the cement floor, the open cage door lead to a long thick trail of some kind that curved and stretched through the shavings. Megan whipped her head to the right and left, making sure her panic was for a good reason. As she eyed the large coiled snakes in each cage she knew she was in trouble, as she kicked the wall on the other side she must have pushed this cage over and in doing so had released some sort of long scaly snake, *most likely venomous*, she convinced herself.

She pulled her head back through the hole and stood in the darkness of the storage unit, shivers ran up her spine as she contemplated what her next move should be. She knew that if she could get to the other wall she could most likely kick through it and move to the next storage unit and possibly get help. She also knew that to kick through the wall she would be forced to lay on her back, on the floor, instantly she pictured her bound legs sticking out of an enormous snake's mouth. *The stomach acids would begin to digest me while I'm still alive,* she thought. She shook her head in defeat, a lump grew in her throat; she had to get out of here.

Megan turned around and began thinking perhaps she should try to bust through the other wall, she could head in that direction instead of going through the snake room, but she remembered that on that side there were at least ten more storage units completing the row, she believed there were only three if she went this way. *And who knows what else I'll find!* She screamed in her mind. She leaned against the wall; warm tears dripped down her face and were absorbed by the cloth tied around her head gagging her. *If the snake eats me no one will hear my screams,* she contemplated. *If I don't get out of here the snake will come through the hole and I'll be stuck with it, either way I'm snake food… might as well get it over with.* She relented.

Shakily, she leaned forward, turned and poked her head through the hole once again; there was no sign of the loose snake. Megan took a deep breath, tucked her head into her chest and fell through the hole, landing sorely on her shoulder in a pile of soggy wood shavings. *Really?!* She screamed in her head. She rolled to the side and wiggled her feet through the hole, trying not to bump any of the other cages. As she made it to her knees she spotted the loose snake, it was lifting its body up the side of the rollup door at the end of the storage unit. The snake had to be close to ten feet long, she decided. It was thick with orange and yellow triangles running the length of its back. The head alone was the size of a small baseball glove. She swallowed loudly, and tried to shake the heebie-jeebies from her body.

As the snake was still occupied she hopped to the other side of the storage unit, cages lined the wall; there was no empty space she could kick through. She counted seven all containing equally large and terrifying serpents and one containing about thirty white mice. *Okay mice or snakes, mice or snakes, yuck…mice…mice running all over me, O…M…G…this can't be happening!* She inhaled deeply, the smell of the snake's urine on her shoulder bit at her nose. *Yuck, okay I can do this and maybe…maybe the mice will lure the snake so it won't eat me! Yes!* She looked at the cage filled with mice, although her hands were bound, her fingers twiddled with nervous apprehension. She snorted as she inhaled a huge breath through her nose. She hopped to the cage with the mice; they all scrambled into a cardboard box inside the cage. She leaned over and rested her chin on the top edge of the cage. Then, with as much power as she could muster, she pulled the cage forward using her head and neck. Pain shot through her face as the metal cage dug into her chin, she didn't care though, and she continued to pull it towards her, away from the wall. Finally the angle was enough and the cage toppled to the floor, slamming into her shins as it did.

"Arrrrrgggg!" she hollered through her gag. She hopped backward allowing the cage to collapse completely onto the floor off of her feet, as she did the cage door popped open. Suddenly a blur of white movement escaped the cage, she watched as the terrified mice ran in all different directions. She turned toward the rollup door and saw that the noise or the vibration of the cage falling had gotten the attention of the loose snake. Its long slender tongue darted in and out of its mouth as it slithered toward her.

"Aaaaahhhh!" she yelled into her gag again, and then hopped to the bare space in the wall, fell to the ground and slammed the sheetrock with her bound feet, just as before it barely made a dent. She rolled her head to the side and saw the snake getting closer, *NO…NO…NO…NO!* She screamed silently. She turned back to the wall and slammed it again with her feet, the dent got a little bigger, again she kicked it; it only dented a fraction more. She looked at the snake again; it was only two feet from her head, she squealed through her gag and slammed her feet into the wall again, nothing happened. *Why isn't this working?! Please, please, please!* She screamed to herself as she kicked again. Her heart pounded in her chest and head, she felt a swirl of dizziness, then she felt a tickle by her thighs, she lifted her head and saw two mice running up her legs onto her belly, she wiggled and screamed, rolling and trying to get them off of her, as she rolled she came face to face with the snake, its long tongue darted out and hit her in the nose, she screamed again in her gag. Her eyes grew wide, fear crawling over every inch of her body, she wiggled herself backward and rolled the opposite direction, as she did she kicked the wall once again, the sheetrock still wouldn't break. Tears poured from her eyes as she continued to log roll as fast as her bound body could away from the snake, it followed her willingly. As her final roll brought her face to face with a cage containing....*what are those snakes again?* She questioned, as it raised its head from its coiled body and thick flaps of skin opened from the sides of its cheeks she screamed again in her gag, she rolled back ward and made contact with the large loose snake, she rolled over the top of it and tried to struggle to her feet. Megan couldn't gain enough balance, tears poured from her eyes she continued to scream into her gag as mice ran by her face and she felt a thick heavy weight raising against her back, she tried to move forward, away from the snake, away from the terror, but she knew there was no way out. The weight of the snake's long body wrapped over her shoulder by her neck, she looked down past her mouth gag and watched as it climbed and circled her body, she screamed again and again and just as she had told herself before, no one heard her.

ৡৣঌ

Lacey swerved into the hospital parking lot and then zoomed under a red canopy labeled "ER". Trent quickly opened the car door and clamored out, just as he closed the door Lacey yelled.

"We'll be back!" and then slammed on the gas pedal, peeling out, causing a burst of smoke and burnt tire in Trent's face.

He coughed then walked through the automatic

doors.

Ben and Lacey flew down the highway in the Baja Beetle; the ride was bumpy as the suspension on the vehicle was designed to handle sand dunes and rugged mountain roads. Ben gripped the edge of the door frame tightly, his knuckles turning white under the pressure.

"Okay, we have two more streets then take a right, then take the third right!" he hollered over the roar of the load engine. Lacey pressed harder on the gas pedal, the beetle instantly jumped forward, as the second right quickly approached Ben tightened his grip, Lacey whipped the car around the corner; other cars honked and waved derogatory sign language in their direction. "Third right! Third right!" Ben yelled to his aunt.

She slowed slightly and bounced into the parking lot of a McDonalds, "Crap! This can't be it!" Lacey yelled, "Where's the next stop?" She quickly yanked the wheel and the Beetle did a tight U-turn in the small parking lot, she zoomed to the edge of the parking lot then slammed on the brakes throwing both her and Ben forward, Ben's seatbelt dug into his shoulder.

"Back to the highway!" Ben commanded.

Anger and terror seemed to wrap Megan's body, as the snake's body did. She looked down to the thick beast trying to coil around her; she looked up to the hole in the wall leading back to Henry's storage unit. She pushed with her feet and rolled onto her belly with the snake now under her. With the volume of the snake's body below her she was able to bring her knees up, she pushed herself onto her knees and slowly wobbled to the wall with the hole, the snake was wrapping tightly around her waist, she stuck her head through the hole in the wall and tried to push the snake off of her body using the wall to push the snake back down her legs and onto the floor behind her. She jumped forward with her head through the wall, as she did her feet tangled with the snake's body and she fell forward, unable to protect her head she smacked it into the concrete floor of Henry's storage unit. Her feet and legs in the air on the other side of the wall, she squealed in pain through her gag as she violently shook her legs trying to get the snake off her lower body.

As she thrashed about her head in one storage unit, her lower body in the other, she heard a loud noise, she couldn't move her head to see where it was coming from but suddenly on her legs she felt a draft of air, she kicked her legs and screamed through her gag again.

"Oh no!" she heard a woman's voice yell, and then felt hands on her thrashing legs. The hands were removing the snake which had wound itself tightly around Megan's thighs. Megan stopped fighting for a second and screamed again through her gag, she could feel blood pooling in her nose from hitting her head on the concrete. "Open A-two!" the voice hollered, with-in a second the metal rollup door was moving noisily open, Megan screamed through her gag once again and watched a shadow stretched across the cement floor.

Two large hands lifted her by the shoulders and pulled her through the hole, as her legs came through a white mouse jumped through the hole as well.

"What on earth?" the man yelled as he took a knife from his pocket and cut the tear and blood stained gag out of Megan's mouth. She coughed with relief and leaned into the man's chest. Huge heaves of fear and exhaustion and terror shook her body as she wept, soaking his shirt. She tasted blood drain down her throat; then felt another hand on her arm.

~ 93 ~

"Are you okay sweetie? Who did this to you? We heard pounding on the wall in the office, we cut the lock off the door as fast as we could!" the woman ran her hands down Megan's head cupping her face as the man cut the bindings off her hands and legs.

"I…I was kidnapped by this guy that's been chasing us," Megan sobbed. "He put me in this storage unit, I thought the light in the other unit was sunlight so I kicked through the wall," Megan paused as she heard the man talking quickly to someone on his phone. "Then I tried to break through that wall but it wouldn't budge."

"That wall separates the storage unit from the main office, oh honey, I'm so glad we heard you." The woman pulled Megan into her arms, suddenly causing Megan to miss her mother even more, she burst into tears.

Sirens and screeching tires forced Megan out of the woman's embrace, suddenly a paramedic ran to Megan and had her sit down while he looked her over and cleaned and bandaged her wounds. A police man interviewed the man and woman who owned the storage complex. A second set of squealing tires forced the police and paramedic to halt their questioning and look outside as a Baja Beetle screeched to halt next to the police car.

The doors flew open and Ben and Lacey ran to Megan.

"Megan, are you okay?" Lacey yelled as she pulled her into a hug.

"She fought off a snake and got pretty banged up. The manager is tracking down the information for the man that rented the storage unit," an officer explained.

Ben jumped toward him, "I can show you where I think he is! He has my sister's phone and I'm tracking it!" He handed the phone to the officer, who immediately pulled his radio from his belt, "His name is Henry!" Ben said loudly talking over the officer who was sending police to the coordinates listed on the phone. The officer smiled and nodded quickly to Ben.

Ben wrapped his arm around Megan as Lacey had her hands properly cleaned and bandaged by the paramedics.

"Did you get the geocache?" Megan asked shakily, wiping a drip from her nose.

"We did, next stop is a shipwreck." Ben smiled at her.

"Wait," Megan looked back to the car, "Where's Trent?"

"Wild boar accident," Ben said matter-of-factly.

"What? Is he okay?"

"Oh yeah, he's at the ER, getting his hand fixed," he clarified. Just then Ben felt something on his leg. He looked down to see a large snake sliding over the top of his sneaker. He jumped in panic and fell backward, screaming until he landed, just as he hit the ground he began crab walking away from the serpent. "Oh, my gosh!" he screamed.

"That's what I was fighting!" Megan yelled as she jumped away from the snake, an officer grabbed the snake's head and yelled for help, two more officers joined him making sure the snake didn't begin to wrap itself around any of them.

Ben climbed to his feet.

"See Ben… terrifying!" Lacey called out from the side of the ambulance.

"Yeah…but I still didn't *pee my pants*!" he hollered back. Lacey turned bright red and hung her head to her chest as the young paramedic bandaging her giggled.

10

As Trent, Megan, Lacey, and Ben exited the airplane everyone in the terminal looked at them oddly, they were a frightening bunch, after all. Ben in his large head-bandage and eye patch, Megan with a large bandage across her forehead from landing on her head when she was trying to escape the snake, both of Lacey's hands were bandaged, and now Trent had a large bandage and cast on his hand as well. They were a sight. On the plane they had all agreed that it was best to tell people they had been in a car accident, if anyone heard the true tale of how this had all happened, they wouldn't have believed it.

"From this website I'm on, it looks like we need a four wheel drive vehicle to get to the beach where this shipwreck is," Ben said as he played with his phone. "Think you can drive with your hands like that Lacey?"

"Oh yeah, I drove on Molokai, just yesterday," she replied.

"Uh…yes, I guess I should have asked if you could drive us *safely*, you nearly killed us yesterday, it would be horribly ironic if after all of the near death experiences we've had for us to actually die in a boring car accident." Ben laughed.

"I'm fine!" she growled back.

"Wow!" Ben said sarcastically. "Okay then, let's get this done!" he said as he walked to the sliding doors and onto the sidewalk.

∝∽

The bright white sand almost blinded Ben as he stepped out of the Jeep. The sea was a bright teal, with black and white rocks protruding from the wavy surface. Snorkelers could be seen floating in the water, occasionally blowing water out, just as a whale would clear its blow hole. This looked, felt, and even smelled like paradise, Ben thought. He took in every beautiful element around him, including a large rock that had *Shipwreck Beach* engraved into it. He quickly snapped a picture with his phone.

Ben began walking toward the beach, the group following closely behind, "Okay, so I think we definitely have to go in the water, the coordinates are, 20°55'16.10" North and 156°54'36.22" West," he said as he walked. "Which means it's out about one hundred feet in the water I think." He put his phone down and looked all around; then peering around a small outcropping cliff he saw an enormous rusted, dilapidated ship, resting eerily in the water. The stark color contrast between the bright teal water and splashing white caps compared to the ship's burnt rusty skeleton was transfixing. Once they looked toward the ship, they couldn't take their eyes off of it.

"Definitely the place, let's get our gear on and see

~ 97 ~

if we can do this," Ben said as he pulled two swimming caps out of his pack and handed one to Megan. "Can't get our wounds wet, we're gonna look like the biggest bunch of nerds!" he laughed. Carefully he covered his head with the swimming cap, and then donned a large face mask that covered his eye patch and other bandage.

Lacey and Trent had both put thick plastic bags over their hands and sealed them off with rubber bands above their elbows, already people were looking their way, wondering what on earth they were doing.

"Nothing to see here, people; go about your business!" Ben called out jokingly. The group waddled to the water in their snorkel gear, with their flippers slapping the sand as they prodded to the shoreline.

The ship wasn't very far out in the water, it was enormous, Ben had read that it had been a cargo ship that was deposited here and just never removed. As they pulled themselves through the water bright fish and sea turtles danced around them. Swimming flawlessly and almost unaware of the invasion, they ate and played, it was a completely different world under the surface. Once close enough to the ship they felt the drop in temperature, the shadow of the large vessel created a chilly zone, it felt as though they were suddenly in a different ocean.

The rusted metal of the hull was covered in sea urchins and anemones, star fish of every color created a brilliant canvas under the water. These creatures had made their homes on this ship; all around it life flourished, in the shaded waters a different variety of fish could be seen, not one going outside the barrier of the ship's shadow. The blues and yellows, greens and oranges of the fish's sleek bodies were incredible, colors Ben didn't realize even existed in nature, thrived here.

The group floated amongst the glorious sea creatures effortlessly for over twenty minutes, it was easy to get lost in the wonder in a place such as this. Finally Ben pulled himself alongside Megan, Lacey, and Trent, and motioned for them to follow him past the long body of the ship to the rear propellers. The sea was rougher at the back of the ship; small waves broke and crashed on the ship's rusty surface. The group bobbed and tried to maintain their buoyancy in the rougher waters while Ben looked on his phone to get a more accurate location of the geocache. As he extended his hand toward the ten foot tall propellers, indicating the geocache must be inside, the entire group seemed to sigh with anxiety.

They all stared at one another, no one wanting any more injuries, but also not wanting anyone else to become injured. It was a paradox of self-preservation versus a sense of responsibility to the group. Finally Megan removed her snorkel mouth piece and spoke up, "I can go in," she said as she moved closer to the massive circular propeller. Trent and Lacey looked at each other, they both knew they wouldn't be good candidates because of their hands; not having the ability to grasp with both hands could be fatal when maneuvering around the sharp blades, especially in the rough waters.

"Okay," Trent said, "We'll give you two minutes." Ben nodded in agreement, as much as he wanted to retrieve the geocache and see the inner workings of the propellers, he was having a hard time seeing out of his one eye and holding his breath. With every attempt to plunge under the water his head pounded to the point of nausea.

Megan put her mouth piece back in and carefully moved closer to the propellers. The curved rusted steel blades looked like a piece of art in the bright blue waters.

As the waves crashed and foamed millions of air bubbles whooshed and curved around the blades as they moved toward the surface. Megan grasped onto one of the propellers and carefully moved her head in between it and the propeller blade above it; she could barely fit through the blades, which made it all the more clear to the group that she was indeed the only candidate for the job.

She looked back toward the group and waved, then carefully pulled her body through the slight opening. Inside the massive circular area, behind the propeller were thousands of fish, they all swam toward her and then escaped out of the propeller blades. Megan held her breath as her snorkel piece was now completely submerged. She looked around the strange alien environment. Debris of all sorts had deposited itself within the housing of the propeller. The long iron axel rod which connected to the propeller was covered with seaweed, rope, fishing line, and gunk. Megan looked upward and noticed that there may be a small air pocket at the top of the space. She moved up carefully, once she felt her snorkel rise out of the water she blew a burst of air through her mouth to clear her snorkel, water and air spewed out over her. Once her snorkel was clear she inhaled the moist salty air from the air pocket in the propeller cylinder. The taste of the air nearly made her gag, but the burn in her lungs was quickly relieved and made the flavor much more bearable.

As she bobbed in the water and took a few more breaths she noticed a small black box wedged between the propeller rod gearing. She quickly moved under the water to investigate. It was clearly the geocache, but it was wedged so tightly she wasn't sure how she could release it. She moved her small hands around it, pulling and wiggling the box, but nothing happened. Finally she realized that if the propeller moved it would force the box out of the gearing. She swam to the propeller and began trying to push the blades down; any movement would help un-wedge the box. Unfortunately fifty years of rust and gunk prevented the blades from moving at all, they were almost completely petrified. Megan moved her head between the two upper blades and removed her mouth piece,

"Hey I found it, but it's wedged in the gearing, can you guys try to move the propeller so it will force it out?" Ben, Lacey, and Trent swam closer and all carefully grabbed on to the propeller blades. Trent used only his good hand and Lacey used the backs of her hands to try to manipulate the enormous bladed wheel. Megan inhaled deeply, gaining a new lungful of fresh air, then put her mouth piece back in and swam back to the gearing.

As Ben, Lacey, and Trent pushed on the blades small pieces of rust began to float off the attachment to the rod, the water was turning a gross shade of burnt red, as more debris became loosened. Megan tried to push the floating nastiness away from her face, she knew this was a good sign; there had to be some sort of movement to force the built-up gunk to become free of the mechanisms.

Within two more seconds a huge cloud of rust and filth filled the water, a strange sensation filled the cylinder, Megan was being pulled away from the gearing through the water, suddenly the propeller popped free and moved. With the smallest movement of the rod the gearing turned and all of the sudden the small black box didn't pop free as Megan had originally thought it would, instead it was crushed and pulled through the gearing. Megan gasped as she saw it disappear around a large gear; she inhaled a mouth full of rusty, filthy water, and then had to pull herself to the top air pocket. She choked and coughed out the disgusting water then hollered as she scolded herself, for her idea gone wrong. She put her snorkel back in, unwilling to give up, and lowered herself once again into the murky water. The propeller had stopped moving and the gears were still once again.

Megan carefully reached her hand into the now dark cloudy space of the gearing and felt around for the geocache. On the opposite side of the gear wheel where it had originally been she felt a crumpled, small piece of metal, sticking out from between an upper and lower gear. She grasped it and wiggled it free from the teeth of the two wheels. Holding it close to her face she could see that it was totally squished. It had been flattened by the teeth on the gears as it was pulled through. A sense of defeat filled her chest. As her lungs burned from not only the emotional disappointment but also her need for oxygen she swam to the propeller and pushed herself through the blades. As she surfaced she cleared her snorkel then took a huge breath.

Trent, Lacey, and Ben were still bobbing in the warm, turbulent waters. As she lifted the geocache out of the water, they all stared with confusion. Megan looked at them sheepishly, "So, my plan…uh…didn't work. Sorry guys." She frowned apologetically. Ben moved to her and grabbed the geocache.

"It's okay, Meg, thanks for going in after it." He eyed the crumpled box trying to figure out what to do. "Let's get to the beach and we'll figure out what to do." He gently patted Megan on the shoulder, consoling his little sister.

On shore they all removed their snorkeling gear and their silly plastic bags and swimming caps. Ben's head throbbed when he pulled the cap off, relieving the pressure form the tight rubber cap. He sat quickly before he could pass out from the pain. Trent was manipulating the box trying anything to get the key from the last geocache to open the squished key hole. "Not gonna happen," he said as he tossed it back to Ben.

"Do you think I could pry it open with a crowbar?" Ben asked.

"Maybe, worth a shot," Trent said as he stood. The group marched toward their jeep parked on the edge of the beach.

◈

Trent and Ben stood expectantly at the opening of the service station's garage door while a young mechanic tried to use a crowbar to open the smashed box, he unsuccessfully tried every angle and the box wouldn't budge. "How do you feel about me sawing it?" the young Hawaiian man asked as he gently tossed the box between his hands.

"You can do that? Yeah that would be great!" Ben said enthusiastically. The young man motioned for Ben and Trent to walk with him to the back of the shop. He handed them each a pair of safety glasses.

"Can't afford to lose your other eye, kid," he laughed as he motioned to Ben's eye patch. Ben blushed and put the glasses on. The young man pushed a power switch on a large circular saw, the blade spun to life humming loudly. He then put the box on the cutting table and lowered the saw onto it. An ear splitting noise filled the space as metal met metal and the box was ripped open. As he lifted the saw back up and secured it the box fell into two pieces, when the box split apart so did the key that was inside. "Oh…whoops," the guy said as he picked up the pieces of the key and handed them to Ben.

"It's okay," Ben replied, "We can deal with this." They thanked the man and went back to the car, Ben looked closely at the top of the key, he rolled it in his hand and smiled when he realized the waypoint was still clearly intact. "Time to go to the airport, say *aloha* to Lāna'i," he looked at his cell phone again. "We need to go to, Kaho'olawe, from the aerial pic on my phone there is a big hole in the ground that the Cache Master wants to show us. Let me Google this." Ben settled into his seat as Lacey pulled into traffic and headed toward the airport.

"Okay, well maybe a problem," Ben said as he tapped the screen of his cell phone, "This is also a private island, we have to get permission to go and we can only go by boat, we have to get permission from the 'Protect Kaho'olawe Ohana Commission', if they say yes then they will take us to the island."

"What if they say no?" Megan asked.

"Then we don't go and our trip is over. The Coast Guard patrols the waters in-between Maui and Kaho'olawe, if we try to go by ourselves we'll be arrested."

"Oh, well there goes my idea of sneaking over," Megan relented. Ben manipulated the screen on his cell phone a few more times; then suddenly was speaking to someone.

"Aloha, to you" he said.

"I needed to go to Kaho'olawe to find a geocache located there." His conversation continued, "Yes, yes a geocache... Okay," Ben covered the mouth microphone and swayed back and forth as if dancing, "I'm on hold-hula music," he said to Megan. A moment later he perked up again, "Yes, aloha...yes a geocache, the coordinates? Yes, those are 20°30'15.85" North and 156°40'43.22" West. Yes...Yes, The Cache Master, how did you know?"

Ben asked the person on the other end of the phone. "Well okay, tomorrow morning, 4:00 am. Yes, that is perfect. Thank you, sir." He hung up the phone then announced, "The Cache Master already got permission! It was four years ago, they have been waiting for someone to come!"

"You're kidding," Lacey said.

"Nope, we leave tomorrow morning at 4:00 am, and he said bring Dramamine." Ben closed his eyes and imagined himself on a small boat; his nausea was already so bad the thought of having it be worse was almost unbearable. Just as he drifted to sleep Lacey announced their arrival at the airport.

The twenty foot fishing boat rocked and bobbed in the water. Ben's head felt as though it was in a vice, the pounding was relentless, and his stomach was doing flips and gurgling violently. He closed his eyes in an attempt to escape the pain, suddenly his 2:00am breakfast of a protein bar and Vitamin Water surged into his mouth, he leaned over the boat just in time, and threw up into the rough waters below. Gingerly he sat back down on the scratchy wooden seat, cradling his stomach.

"You okay?" Lacey asked as she handed him a breath mint.

"Yeah, I'll be okay," he assured her. At this point he wasn't really sure if he would be okay, the pounding headaches and nausea hadn't stopped since the accident had happened. The vision in his good eye was constantly obscured by small white and black star like spots; he finally understood what people meant when they said they could see stars after a head injury. Ben closed his eyes again, his only solace being that he had nothing left to throw up.

Within another twenty minutes the engine of the boat slowed and purred loudly behind them. Ben opened his eyes and noticed a long black and yellow raft-like boat, with a large motor on the back. The captain called out to the man on the Zodiac and swung a small rope his way. Once he caught it the two men pulled the boats together. Megan, Trent, and Lacey eagerly climbed over the side of the fishing boat and into the Zodiac. Ben watched as their weight made the Zodiac shake and bounce in the water, he broke into a sweat thinking of being on an even more turbulent water craft. Carefully he climbed over the edge and grabbed Lacey's shoulder, then sat as quickly as he could.

The fishing boat captain anchored the boat and directed the Zodiac Captain to have the group back within an hour. The sun was barely rising, making Ben think this expedition was going to be exceedingly harder in the morning's darkness. He couldn't think about it long though, as the captain switched the motor on and threw the boat into gear the front end lifted up and it surged through the water. Ben felt a wonderful cold spray on his body from the ocean; the mist chilled his body and calmed his nerves. He decided that if his pain continued he would tell his mom as soon as they got back, he would go back to the hospital and see what was going on, for the time being though he had to focus, this was potentially the last geocache.

The Zodiac slowed down as it began to navigate through large rocks and crashing waves, the shoreline was getting closer, although Ben couldn't tell how close due to the lingering darkness and his loss of depth perception.

"Almost there!" the captain yelled, "We're gonna make this quick, so the boat doesn't flip, aint no other way onto the island."

Lacey nodded her understanding, as soon as the boat slid onto the sand she and Trent jumped over the edge and grabbed the front end, pulling it farther onto the rocky beach. The captain handed two flashlights to Megan then motioned for her and Ben to exit. They both willingly climbed over the edge of the boat and yelled thanks.

"No prob, now be back here in forty-five minutes, I don't wanna have to come find you."

"Okay!" Lacey hollered back, then motioned for Ben to lead the way. He stared at the bright screen of his cellphone then pointed to a rocky cliff line just ahead of them.

"Looks like it's just on the other side of the island, this looks like a really narrow outcropping of rocks from the aerial photo, we should be able to get to the spot pretty quick," Ben said as he plowed through the thick sand on his way to the cliff line.

"Heard that before," Lacey said to Megan. She giggled then picked up her pace to be next to Ben.

The large stones that made up the cliff line were black and jagged, like all the other islands this one was created from volcanic activity, evidenced by all the pumice and obsidian that was scattered over the sand and throughout the grasses. As the group walked along the cliff line Ben found a small trail that cut through the stone. The path was well worn and appeared to be the only access point over these intimidating boulders. The group began ascending the pathway in the darkness. The low glow of their flashlight's barely illuminated the tripping hazards along the way, but over the peak they could see the sky lightening - dawn was coming.

When they finally made it to the top the sky

glowed, a deep orange-red color, the choppy ocean appeared calm in the distance, and again Ben was reminded why they called this place paradise, after all their turmoil he had almost forgotten where they were. He had almost forgotten to enjoy the journey.

The group continued single file down the narrow pathway, it cut through a small portion of grassland, the island appeared sparse, there were no inhabitants here, they had been told. They walked toward the sunlight until they reached another slope. The horizon in front of them was incredible, blue crystal waters, with streaks of orange, red, and yellow bouncing off the waves, Ben snapped a picture before looking back to his GPS app on his phone.

"Okay, just another hundred feet ahead," he announced as he looked down the slope. There in the distance he saw an enormous circular bowl shaped crater, "You think that is the caldera or something?" he asked everyone.

"Dunno," Megan replied as she skipped down the slope to reach the crater first. The group followed quickly, not willing to let Megan get too far away with what had happened earlier with Henry. Ben worked his way to the internet on his phone while walking.

"Wow, how crazy!" Ben called out, "It isn't a caldera, it's a hole from the military! After World War Two they practiced with explosives on this island to figure out how much it would take to sink enemy ships, this hole is from five-hundred tons of TNT!" He jogged slowly to catch up.

"Wow, that is crazy," Lacey agreed as she began to walk around the massive hole in the ground.

"Oh, geez, it's kinda sad," Ben added, "When they blew this up, it cracked the cap stone of the island and made it where all the ground water leaks into the ocean, no wonder no one can live here." He shook his head with disappointment. "It's called *Sailor Man's Cap*." He began walking around the lip of the giant crater as well, and couldn't help but feel a sense of grief that this had happened to such a beautiful place. His thoughts wandered.

"I found it! Look it's in the water at the bottom!" she shined her flashlight into the murky rain water that was contained in the hole. As the beam cut through the water it illuminated a small box at the very bottom, "I can get it!" Megan said as she stepped off the edge of the hole and began sliding down into the crater.

"No stopping her," Trent laughed.

Megan's feet hit the water with a splash, "Oh, it kinda stinks," she yelled up to the group. She slid deeper into the water, when she was chest deep her feet finally hit a flat spot. She kicked her feet around as her arms floated, stabilizing her body. As she had interrupted the surface the smell of the water rose up to Ben, Lacey, and Trent. Trent inhaled then coughed,

"Megan, you need to get out of that water, quick!" he yelled down to her.

"Yeah, working on it!" she called back up.

"No, like now, that smells like rotten eggs, like a sulfur gas or something!" Before she could reply Megan dove under the water and grasped the geocache in her hand, she popped up then waded to the inclined edge of the crater.

"Geez! That itches! The water itches!" she complained as she rubbed her arms and legs. "Ben, heads!" she called as she threw the geocache toward him. Ben reached up and grabbed the box from the air. Megan continued to scratch and claw her skin as she climbed the edge of the crater.

"Meg, c'mon, let's get some water on you!" Trent yelled to her as he grabbed a few bottles of drinking water from the backpack on Ben's back. He ran over to where she was climbing out of the crater then immediately started pouring the clean water on her. "You have to be careful, these volcanoes release gases all the time and sulfuric gas can be very dangerous," he said as he rubbed her arms down with fresh water, "Is that helping?"

"Yeah, yeah, sorry. I just really wanted to get the geocache," She explained sullenly.

"No, it's okay, I was just worried about you, 'kay?" he responded. Megan smiled up at him as he continued to pour water over her.

"We'll need a crow bar to open this one; since the key is cut I can't get it in the keyhole," Ben said as he and Lacey hiked over to Trent and Megan.

"You good?" Lacey asked Megan as she rubbed her eyes. Megan nodded with a shy embarrassed look on her face.

"Let's get going then!" Ben announced.

The sun was rising quickly behind them now; the sparkling sea was rough at the shoreline where the Zodiac was still waiting. Ben braced himself for the boat ride back, he was getting closer and closer to breaking down and having his mother take him back to the hospital, but something deep down kept driving him, motivating him to just get one more cache done, he so badly wanted to find an end to this game, but also didn't want it to end. When it ended he would go back to real life. To not having a list of driving commands to keep him occupied and busy, but as his head pounded and his good eye became blurry with stars once again, as the vomit rose into his throat, suddenly going back to a boring relaxing life didn't seem too bad.

11

Ben's mom and dad stared at him; concern was etched into their faces. "Seriously, Mom, Dad...I'm okay. I promise," he pleaded.

"Are you sure?" the melody of Ben's mom's voice rang in his ears. He blinked his eyes a few times, then focused deeper in on her eyes.

"Yes, I'm good, just tired," he replied. The sing song noise in his ears whenever anyone spoke had started on their flight back to the Big Island the day before, he hadn't told anyone about it, but between him looking dazed, pale and continually being plagued with nausea everyone could tell that something wasn't right.

"Okay, then I guess you can go with Trent, your aunt, and sister, but let's change your bandages first," his mother reached over and delicately pulled on the tape covering the gauze on his eye. As she removed the bandage the tension and pain that pounded in his eye socket relinquished momentarily. Ben's shoulders relaxed and he sighed deeply as the pain seemed to melt off his skin. His mother covered his stitches with antibiotic ointment then carefully re- bandaged the area with fresh gauze and tape. "We'll have our phones on, we're staying at the resort so if anything comes up – aaannnnyyyyy...thhiiinnnnnnnnnnggggggg..." her voice began to sing in Ben's ears again, he shook his head and blinked trying to get it to stop. "We'll be here," she continued. She eyed him suspiciously, "Yeah? You okay?" she asked, wide eyed, expectantly, waiting for his response.

He shook his head again and focused hard. "Yeah, mom, I'm good," he said, being careful not to slur his words. *Maybe it's my medicine?* Ben wondered, trying to find any justification possible to shake the worry from his mind. A knock on the door interrupted his thoughts, Lacey, Megan, and Trent walked in before anyone could say, *come in.*

"Sis? He good? Let's get this show on the road!" Ben cringed at the sharp sound of his aunt's voice in his ears. His mother pulled his aunt to the side and gave her some sort of stern warning. Lacey looked over to Ben, concern pulling at the edges of her lips, and then nodded her head, agreeing to whatever his mother was asking of her.

With clean clothes, bandages and fresh water the group walked through the lobby of the resort and headed out into the bright parking lot. The flowers were amazing rainbows of colors, the breeze, faint with the smell of paradise. The fresh air was so rejuvenating Ben felt a new sense of excitement. They all piled into a newly rented SUV and began their way to the Kīlauea Volcano.

As usual, Trent drove as Ben gave him directions;

it was easier to ignore the strange sensations coming from his head and ears if he was focusing on something.

"So, this looks like we're going to some sort of big lava field," Ben announced as he played with the screens on his cell phone. "You'll wanna turn up here," Ben told Trent. Trent turned onto a dirt road and continued driving as Ben instructed.

Outside the window there was smooth black hardened lava for what seemed like miles. A few trees and plants protruded from holes in the hardened surface, but everything appeared to be forever changed by the lava flow.

"It's just up ahead," Ben said. Trent pulled off the road by a brown sign that read, "Pu'u Loa Petroglyphs" Ben quickly typed the name into his phone's search engine. "Wow," he said as he climbed out of the SUV, "This is the biggest petroglyph site in the U.S."

They all walked across a small wooden bridge then onto a dirt path that wound and stretched through the hardened lava. All over the surface of the lava were thousands of ancient drawings and writings, all in native Hawaiian. There were pictures of stick people and animals, some of mountains with smoke billowing out of the top, some of what seemed to be babies. Ben could only imagine what it would be like to write in the thick magma before it hardened.

As he scanned the hardened lava one drawing took his breath away. It wasn't as intricate as the ink that was on all the native's backs on the Forbidden Island, but it was clearly the same drawing. In this picture the giant dragon had lines of smoke coming off of it as it ascended out of a volcano with spewing lava. Ben snapped a picture of it with his cellphone, and then moved on with a new enthusiasm.

"We're going another hundred feet or so, that way." Ben pointed across the lava field, he switched his phone off his GPS app to the camera and documented some of the drawings, the people at United Cellular would love this, he thought.

Although they only had a hundred feet to walk it took them ages to get there. Everyone would stop in awe and wonder as they looked at all the ancient drawings, they could have spent an entire day at this site; it was so mysterious and magical. As they did approach the waypoint all they could see was black hardened stone, there was no geocache and no place for a geocache, unless the Cache Master had removed some of the rock and placed it underneath. The group looked around and agreed that the Cache Master wouldn't have harmed the ancient stone; it just wasn't like him from what they had learned of the man so far.

As Megan wandered around she paused then tilted her head, "Uh… guys, I think I found it!" She took a step back then tilted her head again. Ben, Trent, and Lacey jogged over to her and searched for it. Suddenly all three of them tilted their heads in unison to see what she was seeing. Their eyes grew wide as they saw the numbers carved into the hardened lava, Ben said the numbers out loud as he entered them into his phone, "19°24'16.53" North and 155°16'48.84" West," he waited as his phone downloaded the information. "Sweet, guys, it's close by!" then his face grew confused as he enlarged the aerial photo on his screen. He turned his phone around so the group, who was now hovering next to him, could see what he was seeing.

The picture revealed a large hole in the ground with smoke and steam rising out of it, as he zoomed the photo out red spots of what appeared to be hot lava could be seen, he looked at everyone, "Guys, I think we're going into the volcano."

Everyone looked at each other, then yelled in unison, "Not it!"

❧ ❧

The air was filled with a moist smoke; Megan coughed and sneezed as it tickled her nose. Ben rubbed his good eye as he looked at the vast deep crater in front of them. As they watched the amazing sight in front of them new puffs of smoke appeared as the ground opened up and sprayed debris into the air, showing bright orange and red lava below.

"I don't wanna be a nag or anything, but I think we should ask someone at the observatory how dangerous it is to get really close to the crater," Lacey suggested sheepishly to the group.

"I think that's a great idea," Ben agreed. They all circled around and walked toward a large brown building with huge windows on all sides. Once up the stairs a sign announcing "The U.S. Geological Society" was engraved on the massive door.

The air inside the building was fresh and cool; air conditioning vents lined the ceiling, providing a sweet escape for anyone outside who had been inhaling the humid smoke from the volcano. Tourists looked at various books and informational videos lining one side of the room. On the other side was a tall counter, they walked to the counter and saw a young teenager, with dark messy hair working with five large computer monitors simultaneously.

"Excuse me," Lacey asked, the young boy turned around, he couldn't have been more than twelve, maybe fourteen years old, Ben decided. He walked quickly to the counter. Lacey looked at him, not knowing if he actually worked there or if he was a tourist or something who had just gotten on the wrong side of the counter. "Um…is there someone who works here we could talk to?" she asked.

"Yeah, just a second." the teenager responded. He turned as if he was going to get someone then turned back around and looked at them. Lacey just stood there not understanding the joke. "Zach, Zach Perkins," he said as he extended his hand to Lacey. Lacey looked at him with confusion.

"You, you work here?" she asked.

Zach lowered his hand when she didn't grasp it, and then looked over at his desk and row of computer monitors and in a dry voice replied, "Well, if not, someone's gonna be really upset that my name is on all those reports over there." He smirked to Ben.

"How old are you?" Lacey asked.

"Just turned fourteen, how old are you?" he looked at her genuinely.

"Why?" she asked.

"Oh, I just figured this must be some new introduction technique," he answered, amusement spreading across his young face.

"I'm twenty-three," Lacey replied. "So, uh…you work here?" she asked.

"Yeah." He rolled his eyes annoyed that she was still asking.

"Are you doing like an internship or something for high school?" Lacey prodded, not believing this young kid could run the place.

"I'm working on my PhD," he answered. "Actually right now, I'm wasting my time talking with you people, but thirty seconds ago, I was working on my PhD." He smiled smugly.

"Your PhD… and you're fourteen?" Lacey looked at Trent.

Zach turned to Ben and Megan, "Yes, I'm fourteen and I'm working on my PhD, I'll just pause here and let you think about it before you ask me again," Zach said with yet another witty smile. He looked to Ben and said, "She doesn't seem to understand simple language, is she okay?"

Lacey's lips formed a tight line as her eyes squinted into a glare, "I heard that," she growled at Zach.

He looked at her amusement spreading across his face, "You were supposed to," he responded with a smile.

"Okay, okay, enough, I get it - you're smarter than me, it's not like I'm not used to dealing with overly smart *children*," Lacey said with annoyance as she motioned to Ben and Megan. "Anyways, how close can we get to the volcano?" she asked.

"Well, you're standing on it, so I'd say it's a little too late to ask that question," Zach replied. Lacey glared again, but couldn't help but smile at this kid's wit.

"I mean the crater," she huffed.

"Awe, well that is something different," he motioned for them to walk around the counter, and then turned to the large windows behind him. "Do you see that fence line circling the crater?" he asked as he pointed.

"Yeah," they responded.

"That's how close you can get to the crater," he said in a dry humorous voice. Lacey rolled her eyes at him.

"Is it safe to go beyond the fence line though, like how badly could we get hurt?" she asked.

"Well," he turned looking at the group, he eyed

Ben's gauze covered face and eye patch, Megan's bandaged head and newly acquired welts covering her skin. He looked to Lacey's bandaged hands, and Trent's casted hand. Then he looked directly at Megan this time, "You all seem to be very careful, safety-conscience people, just from my observation," he said sarcastically. Then eyeing Megan's welts said, "I can tell that at least one of you has gotten too close to a volcanic vent or went swimming in stagnant water with sulfuric acid in it." Megan looked up at Trent shyly. "So, I wouldn't *recommend* that you get too close to the volcano's crater." He turned and went back to his computer monitors.

They all turned and walked around the counter, Zach called out over his shoulder, "So I'll be ready to dial 9-1-1, then?"

Ben turned to him, "Yeah man, probably a good idea." he looked at Lacey, "What, it's not rocket science, look at us!" he said as he threw his hands in the air motioning to how ridiculous they all looked.

Zach stood then added, "No, I did rocket science as an undergrad...you guys - figuring you guys out, definitely *not* rocket science," he laughed, "See you on a stretcher in about twenty minutes!" He laughed as he sat back in his chair.

The group exited the building and paused on the front stoop as they read a sign about the "Halemamau" or "the house of everlasting fire." They were about to try to descend into a lake of boiling lava, which was constantly enlarged by steam blasts and collapsing walls.

"We won't be going that deep into the lava right, Ben?" Lacey asked.

Ben pulled the image up on his cell phone again, "No it looks like it is along the edge of the crater about fifteen feet back from the crater itself," he replied.

"Okay, well just to be safe, I want you to wait in the car, I can't risk you getting hurt any worse, your mom will kill me, she told me she would in the hotel room," Lacey said.

"What? That's not fair!" Ben complained.

"I don't care Ben, me getting killed by your mom isn't fair either!"

"She won't really kill you," Ben said.

"I wouldn't put it past her," Megan interjected jokingly.

"You're not going, and that's final." She handed Ben the keys, he tossed his cell phone at her and stomped to the car.

"Okay," she said as she turned to Megan and Trent, "Let's find this thing and get out of here." They all looked at the cell phone then started walking toward the crater. The air temperature rose as they got closer and closer, as they climbed over the wooden perimeter fence the air was so thick with steam and smoke it was hard to breathe. The earth rumbled below their feet with every step it felt as though the ground could cave in. As they got closer and closer to the edge they saw through the thick steamy smoke a large rock in about the place the geocache was supposed to be. Lacey quickly ran to the rock, Trent and Megan followed with their shirts over their mouths and noses trying to filter out some of the smoke.

They circled the rock and found a black box on the crater facing side. There was no key hole, which was good because there had been no key at the last sight. Lacey grabbed the box without thinking then dropped it quickly as it burned her skin.

"Owwwe!" she hollered. Just as she screamed in pain a shrieking sound filled the air and the ground rumbled more violently, the group turned just in time to see a huge steam vent open up five feet from them. As the gases poured out of the vent shards of volcanic rock and tiny flecks of lava flew into the air. Suddenly they were all screaming and running in pain as they swatted at their skin, feeling tiny shards of glass cutting and slicing into them.

Ben saw the commotion and jumped out of the car, he ran to them in a panic. Trent, Lacey, and Megan all jumped over the fence and ran to Ben. They were each covered in hundreds of tiny little cuts that dripped with blood, and their remaining skin was beginning to welt just as Megan's had earlier.

"You guys go to the bathrooms and wash your skin; I'll run and get the geocache! Wait, was it there?" Ben asked.

"Yeah, it's there and it probably has a chunk of my skin on it, luckily my bandages protected most of my hand but my fingertips are scorched." She lifted her fingers for Ben to see. "Go get a sweatshirt, to protect your skin, and some sunglasses to protect...well your good eye," Lacey instructed, "and something else for your hands." She then grabbed Megan's arm and dragged her to the bathroom, Trent followed, waving goodbye to Ben.

Ben trotted to the car and dug through the backseat to find anything that might help. The only thing that could work as a sweatshirt was Megan's bright pink wind breaker, he squeezed into it. He looked for some sunglasses that would provide enough coverage of his good eye, finding none he dug into their snorkeling gear in the back of the SUV. Ben pulled a snorkeling face mask over his eyes and nose, and pulled two neoprene diving gloves onto his hands. He laughed at himself as he realized how he must look.

Ben slowly jogged over to the fence, climbed over and carefully ran to the large rock; the air was thick with smoke and fumes from the volcanic vent just feet from him. He quickly bent behind the large rock and grabbed the geocache. He opened the latch, took the key out and shoved it into his shorts pocket. As he stood, a familiar face stared at him from the other side of the rock. Ben rubbed the ash and dirt off the snorkeling face mask to get a better look at Henry.

"Ben, I want that geocache, give me the money!" Henry yelled.

"Dude, there is no money!" Ben's voice was extra nasally due to the snorkeling mask. He took a step away from the rock and lifted his hands in the air; the bright pink windbreaker was beginning to stick to his skin as the ash fell on it and began melting the fabric. "Look Henry the geocache is right there, there is nothing in it." Henry bent down and grabbed the black metal box, as he lifted it he screamed as it seared his flesh. He looked at Ben and threw the geocache toward him, then held his hands to his stomach in pain. The geocache flew past Ben and landed about a foot behind him, the small amount of pressure from it landing opened up the earth below it. Suddenly another huge amount of steam, ash, and gases spewed out of the new vent, the ground under Ben was beginning to crumble, he lunged forward trying to escape the hole that was almost swallowing him, but couldn't escape. Ben screamed in pain as the earth continued to disappear under him and the steam from the lava below burned the unprotected skin on his legs.

From the observatory Zach noticed the vent opening up, as he scanned with binoculars he saw Ben grasping at the ground trying to escape the vent, he shook his head then hopped over the counter and ran out the door. He jumped off the front stoop then looked around quickly. Over on the side of the building was a tourist helicopter that was used to give volcano tours so visitors could get a close up look at the volcanoes in a safe manner. "This will be *epic*." Zach said to himself as he ran and jumped into the pilot's seat of the helicopter.

He scanned the various buttons and knobs for a split second, then pushed a few buttons and started the rotors. "Just like a video game," he said to himself, and then heard a scream coming from behind him. He turned to see the three rows of passenger seats filled with tourists behind him. They were all wide eyed with fear. "Oh...*hello*," he said shyly, and then decided to just roll with it. As the chopper rose off the ground he grabbed the flight helmet and slipped it over his messy hair, "Testing, one...two," he said into the helmet, then looked back to the passengers who all had large head phones on, they nodded, not knowing if this was really their tour guide or not.

"Well ladies and gentlemen today you will witness something no one has ever seen before. If you look over to the crater of the volcano you'll see that a new vent has formed and in that vent you'll see a young boy." Everyone in the chopper shrieked with horror. "Don't worry now, because this is of course an interactive flight, and so we'll be rescuing said boy." Zach flew the helicopter over to the vent quickly.

"Have you ever done this before?" One of the tourists asked.

"Flown a helicopter, *no*," he answered as he shook his head. The entire group of tourists cried out in fear. Zach smoothly hovered above the steam vent then instructed a man to open the side door and throw a safety rope down for Ben to grab onto. The air in the helicopter thickened as it filled with fumes and smoke. The tourists began coughing and fidgeting, they moved around fearfully in their seats. "Now you'll need to settle down, you'll mess up the balance of the chopper, and this vent isn't an easy thing to hover over, I've actually never seen any of the pilots do this before." This didn't help ease the tourists who were now frozen stiff with fear as the chopper bobbed and shifted over the vent.

Ben looked through the snorkeling mask and saw the chopper cut through the steam and smoke above him, he was hanging onto to the grumbling ground and barely resting his feet on a ledge within the vent. The heat on his lower body was unbearable, his feet felt as though they were on fire, he found himself looking down trying to make sure they were not literally on fire. He moved them a tiny bit and noticed that the soles of his shoes were melting; the rubber was oozing off of the shoes and dripping down into the vent. Suddenly a crushing pain smashed his hands into the hot crumbling earth, he screamed in agony as he looked up and saw Henry standing on his hand, squashing it, twisting his foot trying to make Ben lose his grip and fall into the open hole.

Ben couldn't move his hand, he looked to the side and through his snorkel mask he thought he saw an enormous burst of lava move out of the depths of the hole, it was shaped like a large claw-like foot, with long toes and huge claws. He shook his head not believing his eyes. Suddenly another extreme burst of lava and fire shot out of the vent, in midair it formed an enormous dragon; its wings made of melting lava spread over thirty feet wide reveling a body of pure magma. A long neck of shooting flames twisted and turned in the air and suddenly a huge fanged head appeared. The dragon's mouth opened and shot out a burst of fire as it growled and screamed and hissed an evil bellow. Ben screamed louder and tears formed in his eyes. The dragon's claws pawed at the side of the vent as it crumbled more fiercely beneath Ben's squashed hands. Ben looked again to its face in pure horror, the dragon threw its head once again as it twisted and screamed, and then Ben saw its eyes – they were made of pure blue flames. Instantly Ben's entire body was covered in goose bumps, an incredibly odd sensation considering he was burning to death, he thought.

The dragon flapped its large wings and the lava and flames glowed brightly, but as the cooler air met the lava it cooled it and began turning the tips of the wings into a black cinder. Just as the tips would begin to harden the beast would pull its wings back into the vent covering them with fresh molten lava. The dragon would rise again and flap the enormous liquid wings, flinging bright oozing masses of lava all over the ground.

Ben looked back to Henry to see if he saw it too, the look on Henry's face indicated that yes, he saw it. Henry released Ben and turned to run, just as he did the enormous dragon's fiery claw grabbed him by the back and pulled him into the vent below. Ben thought for sure he was next he screamed louder and begged at the dragon as it flung its wings more forcefully throwing more lava through the air. Its long neck curled down, flames and heat radiating out of the magma made scales that covered its body. The head came twisting and turning toward Ben, and just as it came within a few feet of his face its mouth opened wide, and it began sucking in a mouthful of air, the hissing noise was ear shattering, suddenly Ben didn't know if the rumbling through his body was from the volcano or the growling of the beast in front of him. As it hissed all of the air around Ben was pulled toward the dragon. Like a huge vacuum, it was literally pulling the air out of Ben's lungs as it growled loudly in his face. The heat was burning Ben's flesh and melting the plastic of the snorkeling mask, it encompassed Ben - there was no escape, his stomach churned and he couldn't breathe, his panic and fear were too great. The beast closed its mouth and stared at Ben. Its face glowed and burned a bright red orange, its fangs dripped lava onto the earth below it, and then its eyes burned a brighter blue. Ben couldn't keep his eyes open with the heat. He closed them and then felt something touch his shoulder, he screamed in panic as vomit came into his mouth, every part of his body was failing due to his over whelming fear.

Suddenly he heard a scream coming through the smoke and wind above him and the object on his shoulder moved, he opened his eyes and turned his heard slowly, not knowing if he really wanted to see what was touching him. But he forced himself to look and realized the object was a rope, he turned and stared at the flaming dragon again and then with all his courage he let go of the crumbling molten earth and grabbed the rope. Ben was hanging in the air a few feet from the dragon's large head and then suddenly Zach maneuvered the chopper, pulling Ben away from the beast. The sound of the earth exploding and lava spewing forced Ben to look down as he was flying through the air. Below him the dragon swirled and coiled its long neck and head and dove back into the lake of fire below.

A few seconds later the helicopter hovered by the observatory and Ben let go and dropped a few feet to the ground. Zach slowly landed the chopper a hundred feet away from where Ben was standing. As soon as the chopper's rotors stopped two men came running toward the chopper and grabbed Zach, pulling him out of it. Ben panicked thinking Zach was going to get in trouble for saving him.

He ran to him, peeling the melted jacket and snorkeling mask off his scorched skin as he moved, "Zach! Zach, thank you!" he screamed. The men backed away and allowed Ben to come to Zach.

Zach turned to Ben, and in a voice that was somehow younger and filled with excitement he called to him, "That was *awesome!*" Ben met him and threw his burning arms around his neck.

"You saw it? You saw the dragon?!" he yelled as he hugged him.

Zach pulled him away, "Dragon? What dragon?" he looked at Ben as all of the tourists poured out of the helicopter, "I saw lava, a bunch of it - about to engulf you." Ben stepped back, disappointed, then shrugged as he looked at Zach. Zach looked down to the ground, then pulled his head back up, for a split second Zach's eyes flashed an incredible bright blue color, not just in the cornea, but the entire eye ball, they then returned to their normal hazel brown.

Ben froze and gasped as it happened, wondering if anyone else saw it, his awe was interrupted by Zach, "Like I said, *Benjamin*... that... was... awesome."

Ben was speechless; he nodded as he realized somehow Zach was connected to The Keeper. In total confusion, he turned to the sound of his name being yelled. Lacey, Megan, and Trent were running toward him from around the building.

"Are you okay?" they all screamed.

"Yeah, I'm okay, pretty hot, but okay," Ben said as they hugged him.

Megan pulled her phone out of her pocket and showed it to Ben, on the screen was a picture of Ben being lifted out of the vent by the helicopter, coming out of the vent was a large burst of lava in the shape of a clawed wing. It was right there, frozen on the image. Ben's jaw dropped.

"That's what good siblings do, they document!" she smiled, eyeing Ben knowingly. Ben gasped, and then relaxed a bit, he hadn't just imagined it.

"Sorry you lost the geocache," Lacey said sadly to Ben.

Ben dug in his pocket, "Just the box, not the key." He handed it to her, "You guys see where it leads while I wash my legs off, they are still burning!" he jogged to the restroom.

As he walked out he was surprised to see them all waiting right outside the men's bathroom door. They were all giddy with joy and eagerness. Lacey handed the cellphone to Ben.

He focused on the screen seeing an island, "Which island is this?" he asked as he zoomed in on the picture, then he noticed what looked like a bronze crown and hand, it was hard to see at the angle the picture was at, so he switched modes on the app to get a 360° view, as he circled it around his mouth dropped when the image came in clearer. "The Statue of Liberty!" he almost yelled as he jumped up and down with excitement.

Ben quietly recounted what had happened on the volcano to his parents as they flew over the Pacific Ocean, on their way home, he had assured everyone that their troubles were over as he expressed how he watched Henry being pulled into the vent by a dragon made of fire and lava. His parents looked at one another and smiled, clearly not believing a word coming out of their son's mouth.

After telling the story of how Zach had rescued him, he settled into his seat and closed his eyes, visions of bright blue eyes and wispy gray hair floated in the darkness of his mind. The pounding in his head and noise in his ears became unbearable, yet somehow through the pain he dozed off into a deep sleep.

The flight was uneventful, everyone caught up on much needed rest. As they began their descent into the Medford International Airport, Ben's mom shook his arm to wake him. After a few tries she began to panic and shook him harder, she yelled at him, and then Ben's dad started trying to rouse him. Nothing was working. Finally a flight attendant ran to them to figure out what was going on, she tried and couldn't wake him either, she sat as the plane landed and then had another flight attendant come with smelling salts, when this didn't work they called 9-1-1 and held everyone on the plane until they had unloaded Ben and the rest of his group onto an ambulance.

Once at the hospital Ben was wheeled away with numerous I.V.s connected to his body, his family sat in the waiting room of the ICU for an hour before anyone came to talk with them.

Finally a doctor exited a large doorway, "Are you Ben's family?" he asked.

"Yes," his mother and father stood anxiously, wiping their eyes.

"Ben's experienced a lot of trauma to his brain. I'm assuming this happened when he fell and spilt his head open in Hawaii, did he complain of nausea, pounding headaches, a ringing in his ears and blurry vision?"

"Yes, a little," Lacey said. "But every time we mentioned taking him back to the hospital he said he was fine." She ran a nervous hand through her dark hair.

"Okay, well he may have been okay had you stayed in Hawaii, but the in-flight pressure change made his brain swell, which is what caused his unconsciousness upon landing." He looked at the group bracing them, "We had to induce a coma to allow his brain to go back to its normal size," The entire group gasped in fear. "He's stable right now; we'll keep him in the coma to try to get the swelling in his brain to reduce. Right now we'll have to just wait and see, that's all I can tell you, I'm sorry."

"What if his brain doesn't stop swelling?" Ben's mom asked frantically.

The doctor paused, clearly uncomfortable with his response, "At that point there won't be much we can do." Ben's mom and dad hugged as they sobbed. Lacey ran from the room crying, Megan and Trent followed.

Shortly after Megan returned to the waiting room, "Mom, Dad…are you guys okay?"

"Yes, sweetie, are you okay? How is your head feeling? Do you have any of those symptoms?" they prodded.

"No, no I'm fine, just tired. It sounds like it is going to be a while; can I go home to rest and have Lacey bring me back in a little while? We will also pick up everyone's luggage at the airport." Megan seemed much more mature than her eight years of age.

Her mother hugged her tight, "Yes, you go and rest honey, we'll call you if anything happens." she said as she gently kissed Megan's forehead.

Megan settled into her bed, she hadn't realized how much she had missed it over the last two weeks. After being unable to sleep due to fear about Henry and the relentless adventure of their trip, she quickly drifted off into dreamland. Hours later the phone startled her into consciousness, she ran to the kitchen to find the phone, then realized Lacey had already answered it.

"Okay, thanks, love you too…bye," Lacey said. "That was your mom, they are going to stay at the hospital overnight, and we'll go in tomorrow morning," she said, as she walked over and hugged Megan.

"Where's Trent?" Megan asked.

"He was on the couch…Trent?!" Lacey yelled, but there was no answer. She walked over to the couch and looked around the living room. Then she rushed back into the kitchen and started searching all over the counter.

"Aunt Lacey, what's wrong?" Megan asked.

"The key? Do you have the key?"

"No," replied Megan. Then she looked to the living room and back to the counter and she realized both Trent and the key were gone.

THE END.

∾Waypoint Book Series∾

Waypoint: Cache Quest Oregon
Waypoint: Alaska
Waypoint: Hawaii

Coming soon:

Waypoint: New York

www.waypointbookseries.com

AUTHOR'S NOTE

As always I have left a few spelling and grammatical errors in this book, just a special gift for those of you who love to find them and point them out!
I know they are there, you don't have to tell me or the world about them!

Students were given ten minutes to write a short story, or an introduction to a story, about anything they wanted. The following are the top seven stories chosen. All entries were wonderful and very entertaining.

No editing has been done to any of the submissions. Entries are listed in alphabetical order.

Entry by: Avery Baker

Larry wakes up a sad and scared child. He gets up fast and tries to avoid his father. His father actually forced them into poverty because of his alcohol addiction.

When Larry arrives at school he is known as a "loaner." Most kids avoid him at all cost, Larry is also not that bright.

After school Larry is actually an avid book reader, so like usual Larry goes to the library and he asks the librarian, "Do you have any books about the town's history?" The librarian points him in the right direction.

Larry reaches to the far back of the book shelf and finds a book about the death of his mother. He found it very odd that there was a book about his poor, loving mother. He opens the book and sees that all the pages are blank.

Larry saw this and threw the book to the ground, and briskly walked out of the library. Then Larry ran home to ask his father why this book was so. His father was heavily drunk and screamed at him to go to his room.

Larry ran up to his room to avoid his father beating him. But he still wondered what had happened to his mother, had there been a horrible tragedy?

Entry by: Keith Caldwell

One day Joe was getting ready to go on a trip to the mountains. Joe was twenty-five and just finished his college year to become a stuntman. Joe was packing his bags to practice a new movie clip on snowboarding. He packed all his stuff and got on the road to Mount Shasta with the Hollywood directors to see what Joe has got.

While they are heading to the mountain they see miners by the road blowing up rocks. It didn't concern them so they kept going so they could get to the mountain, because they reserved it for getting the shot. He gets all his gear and goes up Black Diamond. While he is riding up the miners below blow up a rock and the whole lift shakes. Joe was thinking of doing it another day but didn't want to ruin his chances of being a stunt man. They get to the top of the mountain and he starts heading down.

He goes down the first part with ease then tries to spice it up go down all the rails. He hits them all perfect, he goes off the jump. He hits with speed and launches off the hill with a 360° back flip. The directors are impressed. So he gets to a run that is really steep, right when he starts going down the miners blow up another rock but this time it starts and avalanche and he is right below it. With all his skill he is able to get a little farther to get half way down the hill before the avalanche begins to move. Then it catches him, he is moving so fast he trips and falls and the avalanche takes him.

The directors were already downhill so they saw everything and ran. Joe is stuck under 6 feet of snow and can't breathe very well. The minors who started it all check the mountain to see if anyone is there and sees the directors coming down the hill.

Entry by: Aaron Jemmett

I lay in a field of death and decay. My fallen comrades, some were familiar and some were unknown and forgotten. The sight of this place to any man or woman would leave them nauseated and devastated. I know what happened here and nothing good came about war. Nothing was supposed to survive, not even the last blade of grass underfoot. The foe of the human race came and went. The wake of destruction left behind by their ships. The last stand of the rebels, the last chance for humans, was fought here. The final stand of what we are and knew. This is where my story begins, the last known human on the planet.

Entry by: William Noa Taipin

During the freezing cold winter of 2016, Thomas found himself in a very dangerous situation. He was deep in the Himalayas, with nothing but a knife. Thomas was just on his way home to see his mother. When worse came to worse and his pilot suffered from a stroke. Both of them should have died. But for some reason Thomas was meant to survive. Thomas knows he has to find shelter and warmth fast or he will just simply freeze to death. The first few hours are the most important. This is because you still have more energy and warmth than you will ever have. In his mind he knows he has to make a fire and find a way to signal to another plane flying over. His only hope is to use the remains from the plane. So he goes through all of the pieces from the plane and finds that these two wires from the airplane create sparks. So he has his fire starter, now he needs to find something that will burn long enough to keep him warm. He looks around and all he can find left from the crash is a lot of metal and his clothes. The clothes won't burn as long as wood but it will be better than nothing. Thomas takes two extra heavy weighing jackets and lights the bag and his clothes on fire.

After he starts the fire his next thought is food. He doesn't have to worry about water, because of the overabundance of snow. For the next two days he sat next to the slowly deteriorating fire. Just when all hope was gone and he was losing his body to hypothermia, he looks up and sees a hovering rescue helicopter. He then begins floating through the air and falls into a deep sleep.

Entry by: Kipp Pugh

It was a dark night and kids were going into conferences and never coming out. I know this because my friend Tod went to his conference with Mr. Wibble-Waffle and no one could find him afterwards.

I was just about to go to my conference with Mr. Wibble-Waffle with much pleading to my Mom not to go. I told her he would eat our brains and use our skins for his clothes, but she wouldn't listen.

So we went to the school and walked into the classroom and we saw Mr. Wibble-Waffle stroking his cat, Fluffy, on his chair. Right when we sat down the windows were shut by giant metal frames and the door too. Then out of his closet came a huge cauldron, big enough for me and my mom, and my last words were, "Now do you believe me?" Then I was never to be seen again.

Entry by: James Rountree

Since being thrown back in time by Dr. Doom, Iron Heart has been wandering every Mayan city gathering parts and fighting gladiators to build different time machines to get him home. Even though every machine only works with one person in it he made more to make sure he could get home. His plan is to send all the time machines forward in time. If he misses his time period he can use the others to go back and he would slowly work his way back to his own time period. When he gets back he finds that Dr. Doom has taken over the world.

After defeating and conquering one state he takes the survivors to battle Dr. Doom.

Entry by: Danielle Simon

I was running, running as fast as I could. I was running like my life depended on it, because it did.

One week before:

I'm at softball practice. I've been having practice every day except Saturday and Sunday for the past month, from 5pm to 7pm. My team and I have been preparing for a really big softball tournament and it's in two weeks.

My name is Auden Smith and I'm 21. I'm on a very professional soft ball team. I bat 3rd and play 1st base. I've been dreaming about this league and tournament since I was five. Softball is my life.

After practice my friend Isabelle and I go to a coffee shop. Once we have our drinks we sit at a window table. We watch a man all in black walk in, his face is covered too. Lightning fast he pulls out a gun, shoots once and runs out. Nobody knew what was happening until he left. I look over at Isabelle to see if she is okay. What I see is Isabelle with a bullet in her head, and I see the life go out of her eyes.

What happened next is all a blur. Somebody called 911 and they take away her body. I'm still in shock while the police question me. I only realize what happened when I get home. My best friend died, my softball team doesn't have a right fielder anymore. What could happen worse.

I turn on my TV an hour later and see that another person was killed at a bowling alley, and the weird thing is she was on one of the other teams we were to be playing against.

Thank you to all the students who participated in the writing contest!